She knew the ache of unfulfilled desire

And Simone knew the ache of humiliation. How could she have pressed herself against a man she had known for such a short time and do everything but ask that he take her? She sneaked a look at his profile, etched with the arrogant clarity of a silhouette against the green, sunny countryside. He looked severe, the wide mouth held well under control, the softening effect of the cleft in his chin lost from that angle.

Angus turned and caught her survey. Something leapt in his eyes, and his mouth curled. "Don't look so shattered," he said calmly.

Color surged up from Simone's throat. "I am shattered." Her voice was husky. "I don't normally— I mean, I don't..."

The hard twist of his mouth eased into a scarcely less hard smile. "Neither do I," he told her.

ROBYN DONALD lives in northern New Zealand with her husband and children. They love the outdoors and particularly enjoy sailing and stargazing on warm nights. Robyn doesn't remember being taught to read, but rates reading as one of her greatest pleasures, if not a vice. She finds writing intensely rewarding and is continually surprised by the way her characters develop independent lives of their own.

Books by Robyn Donald

HARLEQUIN PRESENTS

HARLEQUIN ROMANCE

Don't miss any of our special offers. Write to us at the following address for information on our newest releases.

Harlequin Reader Service
P.O. Box 1397, Buffalo, NY 14240
Canadian address: P.O. Box 603,
Fort Erie, Ont. L2A 5X3

ROBYN DONALD

Once Bitten, Twice Shy

march 8. 93.

Harlequin Books

TORONTO • NEW YORK • LONDON
AMSTERDAM • PARIS • SYDNEY • HAMBURG
STOCKHOLM • ATHENS • TOKYO • MILAN
MADRID • WARSAW • BUDAPEST • AUCKLAND

Harlequin Presents first edition June 1993
ISBN 0-373-11565-2

Original hardcover edition published in 1992
by Mills & Boon Limited

ONCE BITTEN, TWICE SHY

CHAPTER ONE

SIMONE ATKINSON clung with a slender hand to one of the poles that supported the veranda of the Silver Dollar Saloon, summoned smouldering heat to the famous, tilted green eyes, and tossed her trademark mane of blazing red hair back from her face in a movement as graceful as it was provocative. A low murmur of appreciation rose from the crowded boardwalk.

'OK, Simone, put your hand in the pocket—yes, that's good, arch your back a little—try a pout, yes, lovely...now a big, frank cowgirl's smile...'

The photographer's New Zealand accent was out of place in Virginia City, Nevada, but, for all that she spoke with the same accent, Simone was not. She looked at home anywhere, which was one of the reasons she had made an indecent amount of money modelling all over the world for the last ten years, ever since she had been a raw fifteen-year-old.

Heat sizzled down from a cloudless sky as she postured and posed, using the flirtatiousness she kept so firmly under control in her real life to produce the sultry challenge that was her trademark. She ignored the crowd and the sweat that trickled unpleasantly down her back, ignored everything but the photographer's directions and her own in-built understanding of the clothes she was wearing.

Why was New Zealand, which was sub-tropical, especially the northern peninsula where she lived, never as hot as this? Presumably because it was assailed on both sides by winds from the turbulent Tasman sea and the immense, lonely reaches of the Pacific Ocean.

A wave of homesickness caught her unawares, revealing itself for a moment in her richly passionate face.

5

'Lovely,' the photographer crooned, 'perfect, yes, wonderful. Hold it for a moment… Great, that's great… And that, my darling, is it.'

Straightening up, Simone ran a limp hand over her forehead, blowing out her cheeks in a soundless huff of weariness. 'I think I might die if I don't get something cold to drink,' she murmured.

Instantly an ice-cold bottle of mineral water appeared in the hand of one of the assistants. On a soundless sigh of pleasure, Simone drank over half of it straight down. Then, rolling the cold bottle along the flushed line of her high, perfect cheekbones, she walked across to the hired car that waited for her. Inside it was cool, the air-conditioner humming softly. She grinned her thanks at the driver when he held the door open, and relaxed into the back seat, hidden from interested eyes by the darkened windows.

Eyes such as those of the man who had stood well back in the shadows against the building and watched her with a concentration she found disturbing. During her career she had had to deal with her share of crackpots, but there was something in the way this man stared that sent primitive warnings tingling along her nerves.

Something about the man himself, if it came to that. Not an American, she decided professionally. Although Americans were as disparate as any nation could be, they were also easy enough to pick out, especially if you had the perceptive eye most models developed. No, the tall, very dark man didn't dress like an American. And he did not, she thought, recalling the harsh, masculine face, the impassive observation for five minutes or so before he strode away, he did not behave like an American.

But it was the conviction that she had seen him before, and with that same grimly uncompromising expression, that made her both uneasy and convinced that this man was, like her, a New Zealander.

Not that that would be so surprising. Granted, there were not quite four million of her countrymen, but they were great travellers, and there was usually a Kiwi in any crowd almost anywhere in the world. She had seen him somewhere else, she was sure of it. The rough-hewn contours of his face were familiar to her, as was the striking cleft in his arrogant chin and the mesmerising intensity of that gaze.

Again she endured a silent flutter of sensation, soft as cat's-paws of wind across a still lake—a kind of basic, elemental recognition. Simone listened to her instincts; allied to a relentlessly logical brain, they had been the basis of the very satisfactory position she found herself in now. As the crew packed up she tried to decide why the stranger had made such an impression on her.

Was it his height? He had certainly been tall enough to stand inches above any other man in the crowd. Three, perhaps even four inches above six feet, with shoulders to match. Yet when he had swung away so abruptly it was with a lethal, elemental grace that made her think of mercenaries—those men with coldly practical views about blood-letting and mayhem.

He certainly wasn't handsome. Yet for all that she had seen him for such a short time—and that when she'd been concentrating on her work—she could recall every inch of his face. It had been forceful, hard to read, with strong bone-structure beneath a bronze tan that made him look like some antique homage to strength and endurance. Wavy hair was a deeper shade of the same bronze, his brows black above eyes narrowed against the fierce sun. She hadn't been able to see their colour, but they were dark. He had a straight blade of nose, a wide mouth notable for its total lack of any sort of softness, and that cleft chin that somehow redeemed him from granite imperviousness.

But it wasn't his looks that made him stand out of the crowd. It was a suppressed intensity of emotion, like a flame beneath stone, the molten torrent of lava hidden by opaque basalt—intimidating, yet oddly, powerfully, seductive.

So striking a man should be easy to recall.

Made profoundly uneasy by the slither of apprehension up her spine, Simone deliberately banished the image of the man's face. It was stupid of her to be recalling with such absorbed concentration someone she'd never see again!

'Back to the motel, Ms Simone?'

'Yes, thanks, Brett.' She flashed the driver the smile on which so much of her popularity was based—the slow, sultry, yet somehow self-mocking smile that had first brought her to the notice of a New York model agency, and then to the world. It wasn't a smile she had had to work on; in fact, when her agent had congratulated her on it she had been astonished, for she had just produced her normal way of signifying pleasure. Since then she had read so many accolades, heard so many compliments about it that now she had to strive to take it for granted.

As the car moved quietly up the main street Simone gazed through the darkened windows, admiring the old shops and the saloons, the cheerful throngs of tourists who had come from all over the world to see the small town left over from the bonanza silver-strikes of the last century. Some day, she thought tiredly, she would come back to Virginia City in Nevada and see all the other things she wanted to see now, and didn't have time for.

Another hard, full day here, then two in San Francisco, and then she was on her way home. Ahead of her was September in New Zealand—traditionally the wettest, and often the coldest month of the year in Northland.

'You're mad,' the magazine staff had chorused when she told them she'd be flying back to New Zealand with them. She needed time with her mother, and she enjoyed the slow, reluctant burgeoning of spring, the wild winds and rain interspersed with days of a luminous tenderness, made radiant by the promise of cherry blossom and lambs and daffodils.

From the beginning of October her schedule was full for almost a year, except for the three weeks at widely separated intervals she had kept so she could fly back and see her mother.

She sighed, staring sightlessly out. She would like to spend longer visiting her mother, but it hardly seemed worthwhile, now that Elizabeth Atkinson no longer knew her.

A year from now, she thought with an anticipation that had been building for ten years, looking down with impersonal, professional eyes at the flawless legs that stretched out before her, a year from now she would be home for good. Rich enough not to have to worry about money ever again if she was careful, and with plans made for a full and immensely satisfying future.

At twenty-five, life looked good for Simone Atkinson. Nicely mapped out, hard enough to be a challenge, easy enough to appeal to what she considered the fundamental laziness in her character, but which had been described by her agent as an essentially feline attitude to life. Simone didn't let much worry her; she did what she could to alleviate the rough patches in her life, and, if that wasn't enough, she tried to accept them with grace and courage.

As she accepted her mother's rapid, painless deterioration towards death. It was an aching hurt that was never absent, but she did what she could to make these last years of her mother's life as pleasant as possible, acquiescing with resigned endurance to those things she could not change.

And if sometimes she wept in the night, well, no one, not even the cold, analytical eye of the camera, ever saw traces of the tears the next morning.

The motel was small, but clean and tidy on its ledge above the old mine workings and the dry hills powdered with sagebrush and some sort of conifer. As soon as the

car stopped outside her room the driver sprang athleti-
cally out to open the door. Simone's smile deepened as
she thanked him before climbing bonelessly from the car
to look straight into the eyes of the man who had so
unnerved her at the shoot—the man whose vibrant
energy radiated like dark fire through his tough exterior.

'Ah, Simone, just the person we want to see!' The
magazine's fashion editor, Julia Parr, ruthlessly chic in
spite of the heat, was smiling with something like be-
mused fascination at the man beside her. 'Here's another
Kiwi, for heaven's sake! This is Angus Grey, who
happens to be here on business. Angus, this is Simone,
who comes originally from just north of Auckland but
is a citizen of the world now. Come and have a drink
with us, Simone.'

'Just Simone?' He had a deep voice, made oddly forbidding by a raw note embedded jaggedly in it.

He took her outstretched hand in his. The cool, impersonal touch sizzled right down to her toes as the hairs
on the back of her neck lifted in warning. Simone let
her pale, clear green gaze linger on the strikingly etched
features before limpidly meeting eyes as intensely,
opaquely blue as lapis lazuli.

'Just Simone,' she replied indolently, wondering if he'd
get the message that to her this was a professional in-
troduction, and she had no intention of letting it become
any more personal by telling him her surname.

He did. Blue fire flashed in the depths of his eyes,
was instantly squelched by an iron will.

'Then you must call me Angus,' he said softly, his
wide, severely disciplined mouth quirking at the corner
in a smile as mirthless as it was unsettling.

Just as meaninglessly she smiled back. 'Of course I
will,' she said, her tone leaving her listener in no doubt
that she was conferring an honour.

Julia stared at her, and the uncomfortable realisation
that she was acting like a prima donna almost made her
cringe. However, she held her head high, the lazy little

smile pulling in the lush contours of her mouth. At some subliminal level Angus Grey was trying to intimidate her, but she was not going to knuckle under to the hidden antagonism she sensed behind those severe, autocratic features.

'Come and have a drink,' Julia urged again, doing her best to ease the sudden tension that had so mystifyingly appeared. 'The others are waiting in my unit.'

Simone almost refused. In fact, she had just opened her mouth to say no, when she thought, What am I doing? Why should I let him stop me?

'I'll be with you just as soon as I've taken these clothes off,' she said calmly. 'See you in five minutes.'

And she walked off into the unit that held the accumulation of clothes and other paraphernalia needed for two days of a fashion shoot, feeling that inimical blue regard every step of the way.

'Seen him?' Paula Bishop removed the safety-pin from her mouth and eyed Simone's set face knowingly. 'Yes, I see you have. A sexy beast, isn't he?'

'Julia seems to think so.'

Paula chuckled and helped her out of the denim jacket, the satin blouse that should have looked awful but didn't, and the jeans that made the most of every inch of Simone's long, long legs.

'And Julia's not easily impressed. Didn't do anything for you, hmm?'

Simone shrugged, pushing her hands through the tumbling fire of her hair, easing it away from her flushed, ivory skin. 'He's certainly got what it takes.'

'But you don't want to take it?'

'I don't know the man,' Simone said drily. 'And, contrary to gossip, I don't leap into bed with men I don't know.' She pulled on her own pair of khaki safari shorts and a loose, floating top in cream and coffee, laced tan sandals around her ankles and firmly squashed the stray thought that perhaps she should put a skirt on. Suddenly, in spite of the fact that she had worn the outfit plenty of times, she seemed to be showing too much long, golden leg.

'You don't hit the gossip columns often.' Paula shrugged as she hung up the clothes. 'But if I know anything at all about men I'd say that Angus Grey saw you and decided you were a tasty morsel. I was watching when Julia introduced you. He certainly didn't look at her as though she was an oasis in his personal desert. And, by the same token, he's not accustomed to women turning him down.'

'You know him?'

'Not him. I knew his ex-wife. She was a model too, even looked a little like you, oddly enough. The same colouring, but she didn't have what it takes to get to the top. She was—oh, guarded, I suppose is the best way to describe her. From the way she talked she'd married him for his money, but in some odd way she depended on him. She was afraid of him, too. Always worrying about what he would think or say or do. I thought she was an odd fish. She left him in the end.'

A sinister little chill pulled Simone's skin tight, but she banished it. She didn't care about Angus Grey or his past.

However, whether or not his wife had married him for his money, the Grey man wore an air of bold assurance, that indefinable aura of smoky sexuality that told every woman who saw him that he was good in bed. No doubt he had to push them out of his way with a hay-rake! A prime male animal, she thought disdainfully, removing the earrings that had been dragging down her lobes, and handing them to Paula. But she was not interested in prime male animals, especially not ones who looked at her with a jagged edge of hostility they couldn't quite hide.

'Coming?' she said casually.

Paula grinned. 'Wouldn't miss it for the world. Talk about the clash of the Titans!' She watched Simone walk to the door and said slyly, 'At least you'd be able to wear high heels with him. He must be six feet four, at least five inches taller than you.'

'Give up, Paula.' But she smiled as she said it. For all her gossip Paula was a dear, kind-hearted to a fault. A pleasant change from Julia Parr, who was efficient and professional, but not exactly warm.

To the accompaniment of the other woman's soundless chuckle they left the unit and walked the few steps to Julia's room.

They were all there: Chris Simpson, who was making an international name for himself as a photographer, and so far had been a delight to work with—partly because he hoped that this shoot was going to be his passport out of New Zealand to the really big time; his assistant, the two stylists, and Philippe, who did the hairdressing, along with the make-up expert, Trish Stevens. Julia was perched on the end of one of the beds, laughing up at Grey, who was somehow the focal point of the room. Because he was so big, Simone thought snidely, refusing to accord him any recognition beyond the casual smile she bestowed impartially on everyone.

That eerie, instinctive *frisson* tightened her skin. Drat the man! Who was he, that he could set her on edge just by being in the same room?

'Drink, Simone?' Chris waved a beer can at her. 'Good American stuff.'

She smiled. 'No, I'll have some mineral water if you've got some, otherwise just water with ice.'

'You're *sooo* disciplined,' Sandy Heron, one of the stylists sighed, with an upward glance through her lashes at Angus Grey, who should have looked relaxed but was lounging back in the chair with the stillness of a great hunting animal. Sandy was a little overweight and inclined to be envious of anyone who managed to control their weight without starving.

Simone shrugged. 'No discipline to it. I don't like alcohol, it makes me go all hot and stupid, and pop is too sweet.'

'Then you're lucky,' the stylist retorted.

Chris handed over a glass of icy mineral water. 'Luck doesn't come into it, dearest. As well as being utterly, naturally gorgeous, Simone's a worker.'

Simone lifted her brows, amused yet a little quelling, but said nothing.

Chris lifted his glass of beer and toasted, 'Here's to the most beautiful woman I've ever worked with, and the easiest.'

'The easiest?' His assistant, a young man who was inclined to think ten seconds after he'd spoken, grinned at Simone as she settled gracefully cross-legged on to the other bed. 'A Freudian slip, Chris?'

Chris laughed, not at all averse to be taken as Simone's lover. She shrugged, refusing to join in the teasing game, and drank half her glass of water, relishing its coolness. Before this she had been on location by the Dead Sea, and she didn't think she was ever going to be able to satisfy the resultant thirst.

Across the room her eyes met the enigmatic blue gaze of Angus Grey. He was drinking beer from a can, and he was watching her, his eyes hooded as he lowered the can. His hands were beautiful, the fingers long and lean and dark against the frosted aluminum, with a latent strength that emphasised the will-power she had recognised instantly.

There was something in the way he looked at her, something silently inimical that set her nerves thrumming. This man is dangerous, her instincts warned.

He set the can on the table, and was watching her openly, his expression almost amused, as though he knew exactly what she was thinking and found it funny. Simone stiffened and her chin lifted in unspoken challenge. Deep in those amazing dark eyes something glittered, effortlessly holding her gaze for a long moment.

When a burst of laughter broke the tension, she looked away, blinking to hide her shock and relief. Chris, an excellent raconteur, was telling the story of Simone and the mule that had tried to bite her, threatening to blackmail her with the photographs he'd taken as she'd run ignominiously from the beast's bared yellow teeth.

It was a funny story, and this time it was even funnier than it had been the last time. Her heart thudding as though she had run a hard race, Simone responded with a smile and parried the resultant teasing with her usual easygoing humour.

Then Julia asked, 'And what exactly are you doing here, Angus?'

'I'm on business,' he said. Not curtly, but as though he didn't care to make explanations.

Simone scanned his harshly sculptured face from beneath her lowered lashes. He might not be handsome, but neither was he ugly—far from it! Those terms were just not relevant when it came to Angus Grey. He was—exciting, with a barely hidden underlay of danger. The combination of arrogant masculinity with those stunning eyes, set in black curling lashes that would have flattered any woman, as well as a mouth too rigidly disciplined to be beautiful, was altogether too potent. As she suspected he knew.

Simone's eyes lingered on that mouth. To her horror she found herself wondering what it would feel like on hers. To hide the wash of apricot that stole along her cheekbones she drank some more mineral water, listening intently as he spoke.

'I invent things,' he was saying in answer to Sandy's blunt question. At the exclamations that followed, laughter sprang into the depths of those wonderful eyes.

'Like what?' Julia demanded, when it was obvious he wasn't going to expand.

'Oh, a variety of things. At the moment my brother-in-law and I are interested in solar power.'

'There's another one like you!' Sandy asked rather too lightly. 'Is your wife an inventor too?'

He lifted one of those winged black brows in a devastating way, but said amiably enough, 'I'm not married.

My brother-in-law is married to my sister, and no, he's not an inventor. He's the money man.'

There was something not quite right there. Intrigued, Simone studied him carefully. The deep voice hadn't altered at all, but she picked up a slight rigidity that held his big, lean body a little more erect for a moment. He doesn't get on with his brother-in-law, she decided. And although his brother-in-law might be the money man, even the most cursory glance at Angus Grey's clothes revealed that a lot of it came his way.

'I see.' Julia nodded, clearly prepared to be fascinated by anything Angus Grey did. 'Are you going to make much better solar units, or something?'

'Well, something along those lines.' His smile was easy, practised, and it obviously worked on Julia, but Simone wondered why the woman couldn't see that he was only humouring her. 'I've been over here on and off for the past year finding out what the Americans are doing with their alternative power sources.'

'When do you go home?' Sandy asked, simpering slightly.

His smile was impersonal. 'I'm spending a couple of days looking at wind-power installations around San Francisco, and then I'll be on my way.'

'Are you flying out of San Francisco?' Julia again, her voice too casual.

'Yes.'

She gave him a dazzling smile. 'Then perhaps we'll see you there, or on the plane home.'

He smiled back, and the hidden charm blazed forth, a flash of sexual magnetism made infinitely more potent by the contrast to his cool aloofness. 'Possibly,' he said non-committally, managing to sound at once aloof, yet without offending by any obvious rebuff.

Simone's eyes narrowed a fraction, then her lashes swept down. Was his charm deliberate? She suspected it was, although it had none of the specious tarnish she had seen in other men who thought that charm was enough. Like Jason.

A shudder of foreboding chased its icy way across her skin. She sat very still, barely breathing, until the pain caused by her dead husband's memory receded. Hastily she recalled other men who possessed that effortless, potent attraction. It was not a common attribute, but she had met some; Caine Fleming, another New Zealander and a friend, was one, and there was an English lawyer she had met several years ago, as well as a gaucho she had met on a shoot in Argentina, a Japanese businessman...

Each time she had recognised that basic attraction, but for various reasons it had been impossible, and she had not allowed herself to dream dreams about any of them.

And she was not, she decided with the hard practicality that was as much a part of her character as her refusal to take either herself or her hectic life seriously, she was not going to dream any dreams about this man, either.

Latent beneath Angus Grey's charm and the vital, male magnetism she sensed an unsettling intensity that could, she suspected, become fanaticism. Simone had her reasons for being afraid of men whose guarded expressions hid private, uncontrollable demons; she had married one. Jason had left her badly burnt, and with a determination never again to be held to ransom by ungovernable emotions.

Angus Grey was nothing like the man who had hurt her so badly, but she sensed in him the same power to maim and destroy. A dangerous man, she thought again as he said something that made everyone laugh.

She said little, giving her best impersonation of a sleepy, not-too-bright model, content to be admired for the body and face a kind set of genes had handed to her. Everyone was a little elevated, as though it were the last day of the shoot instead of the first. It was, she realised with an enormous reluctance, because Angus Grey was there. He had the power to excite people just by his presence.

Simone discovered in herself a vast curiosity about him that alarmed her, but didn't stop her speculation. How old was he? About thirty, she guessed—a very mature, self-contained thirty. Perhaps a couple of years older, but no more.

'So,' Julia said, looking very pleased with herself, bringing to an end the discussion on where to eat, 'shall we eat at this Basque restaurant, then? It sounds fascinating.'

There was a chorus of agreement. 'Angus?' Julia asked, raising her brows at him.

He shrugged. 'Yes.'

'Are you going back to Reno tonight?'

He shook his bronze head. 'I'm staying here.'

'Oh, lovely.' Julia smiled, not even trying to hide her delight. Looking around the room, she suggested, 'Shall we meet here in half an hour, then?'

Angus Grey's glance slid to meet Simone's. 'Can we all be ready in such a short time?' he asked, his mouth quirking sardonically.

She gave him her laziest, most impudent smile, fluttering her lashes in a parody of flirtatiousness. 'Are you insinuating that I take an hour to make up my face?' she asked with a purring sweetness he had to know was specious.

Not intimidated, as so many men were by her, he grinned, showing strong white teeth. One straight brow lifted. 'Do you?'

'No,' she said, joining in the laughter from everyone around.

'When she's not working she doesn't wear make-up,' Julia explained, making a joke of her disgruntlement. 'What you see there, Angus, is what you get, God help the rest of us women. If she weren't so nice we'd all hate her.'

'Speak for yourself,' Chris said, running a slightly possessive hand over Simone's shoulder. 'I can't think of a single red-blooded male who'd hate Simone.'

Still smiling, Simone uncurled. No one would have known that she was angry, both with Chris and with Angus Grey. 'Half an hour,' she said, yawning. 'Right. Time enough for a nap.'

Everyone laughed again, except for Angus Grey, who was watching her with a narrow-eyed concentration that sent her pulse-rate up.

'She's an expert at sleeping,' Julia told him, after a quick glance at Simone's lovely, blandly unruffled face.

'I need at lot of it.' Simone bestowed a slow smile around the room. 'See you later.'

She chose a dress the colour of old ivory, sleeveless, long-waisted, crossed over at the back to bare the elegant line of her spine. Her brilliant hair, a true flame-red, flowed in a sea of crinkly waves to her shoulder-blades. She looked, she decided, just right—cool, serene, a little unapproachable.

Just the way she wanted to look. Angus Grey—and Chris—should get the message.

Not that she was worried. She had had some experience of dealing with photographers who fell in lust with models' faces and bodies. Chris would be easy enough to cope with. And in spite of the mutual awareness that had so annoyed them both she didn't think she had any reason to worry about Angus Grey, either. The man clearly didn't like her. Which was fine by her, because she didn't think she liked him, anyway.

However, she was determined to reinforce her unavailability. Many men had strange ideas about models, imagining that using one's body to sell clothes implied that the owner of that body was amenable to selling it for other purposes.

Simone was not naïve; there were models who had a cheerfully amoral attitude to sex, but she was not one of them. She had been a virgin when she married Jason

Sinclair at the age of nineteen, and after that experience she had been in no hurry to offer herself to any other man.

As usual, she was the first ready. She hesitated a moment at the door, sucking in her breath as the heated air struck her like a blow, but the curiosity that made her enjoy location shoots impelled her forward. The motel faced east from one of the ledges beneath the mountain overlooking the town. There was a wall there, low enough for her to be able to see out over the valley and the hills beyond to a distant stretch of plain, obviously irrigated. Even muted by distance the green flats contrasted shockingly with the prevailing colours around her—tawny hills scattered with the dusty green of some sort of conifer and the silver that had to be sagebrush, surely?

She stood taking it all in, trying to impress the contours and colours on to her brain, her eyes fiercely intent, until her prickling skin warned her of someone's noiseless approach. 'You'll get burned,' Angus Grey said from behind her.

'The sun is almost behind the hill.' She didn't turn her head, but the eyes that were fixed so firmly on the landscape saw nothing now. 'Besides, I'm lucky. I don't burn easily.'

Silently, like a shadow slipping through the hidden reaches of her soul, he moved to stand beside her. In that deep voice with the implacable note abrading it, he asked, 'Are you going to be in San Francisco too, Simone?'

'Yes.' Her voice was dry and brisk. 'And on the plane home as well.'

'Are you based in Auckland?'

The questions seemed casual, as though he was merely making conversation, but she didn't think that Angus Grey had ever been casual in his life. 'No, in New York, but I spend a month at home each year.'

'Will you be skiing?'

Irony tinged her voice. 'No.'

She would spend the month with her mother, who was unable to walk, unable to talk, unable to laugh and dance and flirt, to enjoy all the things she had only dreamed of until she'd sent her daughter's photograph in to a competition, and found that a fifteen-year-old could earn enough to provide her mother with all the glamour and excitement she had ever yearned for. But Elizabeth Atkinson didn't crave it now. A premature victim of Alzheimer's disease, she lived now in some private, enclosed world, unable to break out, no longer craving the stimulus she had once so greedily embraced.

'You don't like skiing? Or perhaps,' he said, the smooth tone failing to hide the acid in the words, 'you prefer less strenuous sports.'

The antagonism that crackled between them came just as much from Simone as it did from him, and she was opening her mouth to make a sharp counter-attack when common sense prevailed. All she had to do was last out this evening, and she'd never see him again.

Her magnificent shoulders moved in a slight, dismissive shrug. 'I like skiing well enough,' she said with supreme indifference. 'How about you?'

They were interrupted by a welcome voice. 'Ah, there you are,' Julia observed, her eyes sliding from one shuttered face to the other. 'All ready to go, I see.'

Simone made no effort to hide her pleasure at the interruption. Smiling lazily at the editor, she turned away from Angus Grey and left them, joining the rest of the crew in the courtyard.

An hour and a half later she was listening to Julia moan, 'Oh, God, if this was how the Basques ate they must have rolled down these hills and bounced up the other side. What an enormous meal! Simone, how can you eat your way through all that?'

Simone grinned. 'I have hollow legs,' she said, surveying the ruins of the spicy rabbit on her plate with regretful pleasure.

'It's maddening. Why can't you be like everyone else and get fat?'

'Because she's a thoroughbred,' Chris informed them in a slightly slurred voice. Already on his fourth glass of wine, he was getting more blatantly suggestive with each one. He leaned forward and eyed Simone's breasts beneath the thin ivory cotton. 'In all the right places,' he finished significantly.

Simone could have hit him, especially when out of the corner of her eye she caught the sardonic expression on Angus's lean face. However, she said calmly, 'Thanks for the appreciation, Chris, but don't you think there's something just a little sexist about remarks like that?'

'Oh, you can admire my attributes any time,' he leered.

She lifted her brows. 'Would you like that to be the only thing I admired about you?' she asked directly.

He smiled foolishly, but one of the stylists said something to him and he turned away. Carefully avoiding Angus Grey's gaze, Simone looked around. Almost all the tables in the restaurant were full. Apparently Basque meals were popular in Virginia City. Although several men smiled at her, with the smoothness of long experience she caught nobody's eye, turning her attention back to their table.

Angus Grey was sitting opposite, oppressing her with his presence. She felt stupid and tired, her eyes gritty with exhaustion. It was past her usual bedtime, and she wanted nothing more than to be stretched out between clean sheets, enjoying the last, drowsy moments of consciousness before sleep claimed her.

But everyone else was having a wonderful time.

So she stuck it out until they decided to call it a day, although she refused Chris's offer of a drink in the bar afterwards. He and one of the stylists decided to stay, but the rest of them walked back together. Even though the sun had gone down it was still hot outside, probably due to the warm wind blowing up from the valley and around the hills.

Julia and Angus Grey walked a little behind the main group; Simone was irritated by the fashion editor's laughter, warm and intimate, and the deep tones of the man's voice, just too distant to be able to discern what he was saying. Whatever, Julia was loving it, she thought waspishly, rubbed raw by some profound, inchoate restlessness.

Once back at the motel she went straight into her unit, able to breathe calmly once more. Drat the man, he had no right or reason to look at her as though she were something that had crawled up from the swamp.

She had just washed her face when a knock on the door brought her thin brown brows together.

'Miss Simone?' the motel owner said, her back to the mildly noisy group still talking in the courtyard.

'Yes?'

'Got a message for you from New York. Can you ring your agent right away?'

It was ten o'clock here, which meant that Thea Peacock would normally be asleep.

'Says it's important,' the proprietor said, understanding the quick look Simone had given to her watch.

Simone sighed. 'Thank you very much.'

When she got through it was with dawning alarm that she heard her agent's soft voice. Thea said, 'I've got bad news for you, I'm afraid, honey. Is there anyone there with you?'

'What—is it Mum?'

'Yes. The nursing home rang.' A pause, then Thea said bluntly, 'She died two hours ago. I'm sorry.'

Simone stared unseeingly at the wall, clutching the telephone with frozen fingers. Swallowing, she asked in a thin voice, 'What happened? A few days ago when I talked to the matron she told me Mum was fine.'

'Pneumonia, apparently. It was quick and painless, they said.'

'I see.' Her tone was remote, without emotion. 'Thanks for letting me know, Thea.'

'I'm sorry, honey. It's useless telling you you'll get over it, but you will, you know. I won't even tell you that it's a blessed release, but that's true, too.'

'Yes, I know. Thanks.' Simone's voice was toneless, her eyes dark and shadowed with pain.

'What are you going to do?' Thea asked. 'I could fly out...'

'No, it's sweet of you, but I'll just get back home as quickly as I can.'

Thea yawned, and apologised. 'Do you want me to deal with the shoot you're on now?'

'No, I'll see Julia first. Thanks, Thea.'

'Oh, hell, I'm sorry it's such bad news. If there's anything I can do—and I mean that, Simone—let me know, won't you?'

'Yes, I will. Thank you.'

'Take care of yourself, honey.'

Simone replaced the telephone and sat for a long time, staring at the wall. Because her mother had been failing for some time the news came as no great shock, but she had hoped to be able to spend this next month with her. Sudden tears burned in her eyes, but she forced them back. She had a lot to do before she could allow herself the luxury of weeping.

Moving with dragging feet, she went out into the windy, hot night to knock on Julia's door.

'Who is it?'

'Simone. It's important, Julia.'

'Oh.' There was a pause, before Julia opened the door. She was not alone. Superbly self-confident, Angus Grey was there, pouring whisky into two glasses. He looked up as the door opened, but kept pouring, his hand steady.

'Angus decided to have a farewell drink,' Julia said shortly.

Simone nodded without interest, rubbing a hand across her eyes. 'Can I see you? Alone?'

Another hesitation, before Julia came out, carefully closing the door behind her. 'What is it?' she asked, still a little brusque.

'I've just heard that my mother has died,' Simone said, controlling her grief into an overriding bleakness. 'I want to get home as soon as I can, so——'

'Oh, God, I'm sorry. What bad luck, Simone.' Julia bit her lip, obviously considering.

'I wondered if you could get another girl——'

Julia shook her head. 'I suppose I could, although it would make things bloody difficult. We're building this whole issue around you. Oh, God, that sounds unfeeling, doesn't it? Hang on while I think.' She frowned, while Simone stood passively by. 'Listen, could you give us tomorrow? If we worked our tails off we could probably get enough done then to get us through. And I can organise someone to take your place in San Francisco. How would that be?'

Simone said, 'I suppose——'

Julia interrupted, 'Do you have to make the arrangements? For the funeral, and all that?'

Tears glimmered deep in Simone's eyes. 'No. I left everything—last time I was home I organised everything. Just in case.' She blew her nose.

'I'm so sorry,' Julia said helplessly. 'I know how close you were. It's a bitch of a thing to happen to anyone, and especially someone as lively as your mother used to be. Can you give us tomorrow?'

Simone wanted to shout that of course she couldn't, she was going home as fast as she could, but she didn't. She was a professional, and there were others to think of besides herself. Chris might be a pain in the neck, but he was an excellent photographer, and he deserved his chance. And the magazine had sunk a lot of money into this shoot. She owed them tomorrow.

'All right,' she agreed, not quite steadily.

'Good girl. And if there's anything we can do...' The older woman's voice tailed away.

Simone gave her a wintry smile, said, 'Thank you,' and walked away.

Back in her room she rang through to the rest home and asked the details of her mother's illness and death, holding back an aching emptiness as the brisk voice of the matron told her that it had been unexpected but peaceful, there was nothing she could have done even if she had been there, and that everything was in train as she had arranged.

Simone set the receiver down with a shaking hand, biting her lip. She wanted to cry. She wanted to get back to New Zealand as fast as she could. Instead she was going to take a sleeping pill, one of the new ones that didn't leave you heavy-eyed and sluggish the next morning, so that she got a decent night's sleep, ready for work.

However, before the pill brought its blessed oblivion, she was going to have to change her travel plans. Her face set in desolate lines, she picked up the receiver again.

It was three-quarters of an hour later before she was able to go to bed, but she had a small plane chartered for the following evening to take her to San Francisco in time to catch the late plane to New Zealand.

The next morning she was up early, her expression aloof and controlled as she got together all of the things that she needed. It was impossible to put her mother's death from her mind, but she was going to have to try, so that she would be able to do justice to the day's work. In the rich golden flood of the sunlight she went outside and got into the car. Julia joined her there, in a subdued mood, although her gaze was shrewdly professional as she scanned Simone's face.

'I feel a heel,' she confessed. 'But this is important— I wouldn't have asked you to stay if it hadn't been.'

'It's all right.'

'It's not, but you're a sweet thing to agree. Now, today is going to be a bit hectic, I'm afraid. Chris has this thing about photographing you in front of an old mine building, and I must admit they're very dramatic and austere, especially with those wonderful dry hills in the background. It'll go really well with the flowing, Bedouin look that's going to be all the rage this summer. Then there's the train ride. It should be fun...' Her voice tailed away as she realised how inappropriate her words were.

Simone donned the bright mask of her professional persona and smiled.

CHAPTER TWO

IT WASN'T fun. It was hot, and the wind tore at Simone's face and her hair and her nerves, warm and elementally persistent, making it difficult for her to concentrate. Grief ate into her concentration, backed by the bitter, guilty query: had she done enough for her mother?

As they were finishing the last shots in front of the mine building, Angus Grey came strolling down the dry, dusty track. He looked thoroughly at home, Simone realised with a small shock. A hundred years ago he could have lived in this sparse, stark land, taken from it what he needed, and gone on his way, unconquered. He had that aura of power, of competence, the in-built arrogance of a man who had complete confidence in himself.

Again that nagging sense of familiarity tugged at her. But they couldn't have met before; surely he would have said something if they had? And he was not, she admitted with a painful honesty, the sort of man you forgot.

'Ah, Angus, you did come.' Julia beamed at him, clearly not in the least worried about showing her interest. Had he spent the night with her?

Chris's voice dragged Simone's attention away from the two who stood talking to each other with such casual ease.

'OK, sweetheart, how about walking out on to that old piece of track? Yes, that's it, over there.'

'I don't like to quibble,' Simone observed calmly, 'but that sign says "Danger".'

'It looks solid enough to me.' He handed his camera over to his assistant and walked out on to the narrow stretch of iron, bouncing up and down on it experimentally. 'Solid as a rock,' he declared.

Simone watched closely, then shrugged. It had shown no signs of giving way. 'OK, but if I break a leg you're in trouble,' she threatened as she walked carefully out.

The track had once run along the side of the hill from the dark mouth of a mine fifty or so metres away to the edge of the bank, no doubt carrying ore to some sort of transporting system. Most of it was long gone, including the supports that held the outer rail, so that the remnant of track was anchored only on one side. The ground under the other had been carried away at some time by a small landslide; the outer rail was suspended over a fifteen-foot drop.

Simone swallowed. It was wide enough to support her, but if she tripped she was going to fall quite a way on to ground not only too far away but altogether too solid.

Forget that there's a drop, she advised herself with a hardiness gained from numerous similar occasions. Photographers could be sadists. Fixing her smile firmly to her lips, she picked her way across the track before turning to face the crew.

'Yep, lovely,' Chris crooned. 'Oh, yes, haul that skirt out and let the wind catch it—yes, perfect, perfect, perfect, darling. Right, just keep that pose...'

But as she felt the skirt rip through her fingers and fly free, she saw a laughing Julia lift a hand to Angus's cheek. Her foot slipped. She swayed, and one of the assistants yelled, 'Look out!'

The sudden cry, shocking in the hot, silent air, finished off what her moment's inattention had begun. Her foot slid through the rail and she fell awkwardly, the hot metal slapping across her solar plexus, winding her. For a moment she lay gasping, the tawny hills spinning about her while she struggled for breath.

The next instant she was being held still by iron hands on her shoulders, and Angus said urgently, 'It's all right, I've got you, just concentrate on getting your breath back.'

She dragged air into her lungs, striving desperately to regain possession of her faculties. Slowly the hideous whirling settled down, and she was able to breathe again. The hot metal across her midriff seared right through the cotton sunfrock, the sun beat down on her unprotected shoulders. Still dragging in her breath, she lay still in the amazingly comforting grip that held her secure.

After a short while he said, 'Do you think you can get up now?'

'Yes.'

His hands were calloused and hard, the hands of a man who did hard physical labour, but they were surprisingly gentle as he helped her to her feet and supported her back to safety.

The crew had been standing around, staring down at her, their comments a babble of noise, but now Julia demanded, 'Are you all right?'

Simone asked, 'How's my face?'

She got a narrow-eyed stare from the man who supported her. 'Beautiful as ever,' he said snidely. 'You haven't damaged anything, or even got it dirty.'

She could have told him that it had taken Trish Stevens almost an hour to get this face done, and they didn't have time to do it all again, but she didn't. She was angry, and she was too conscious of the swift shudder of awareness that was stinging through her nerves. He might be an arrogant, supercilious pain in the neck, but, for all that, she was helpless in the throes of a powerful physical attraction.

'Thank you,' she said coolly, stepping back so that he had to let her go.

His smile gleamed white in his dark face. 'My pleasure,' he replied, not trying to hide the taunting note in the words.

Paula Bishop broke in, demanding to know whether the dress was marked in any way. Simone's reassurance was interrupted by Chris's voice, gleefully informing her that he had more photos to blackmail her with, until

Julia, interrupting in her turn, said sharply, 'Really, Simone, you could be a little more careful. That outfit's a designer fashion, and it's too expensive to roll around the dirt in!'

'Sorry,' Simone said amiably, rubbing the arm she had somehow managed to hurt on the rail.

'Well, at least we don't have to worry about bruises,' Julia said crisply. 'We've finished with all the swimsuits, thank God. OK, let's get going, we've got a lot more to do today.'

Angus had stood back as they flocked around, but he asked now, low and fast and clipped, 'Are you hurt at all?'

'No.' Simone smiled rather ironically. 'No, not a bit.'

Julia looked a little shamefaced. 'Of course she's not hurt,' she said crisply. 'Come on, Simone, let's get going. It's the train next.'

The train was wonderful. It had a delicious whistle, and looked as though it had come out of every Western Simone had ever seen. All it needed was a gunslinger or two.

On each of the three trips they took on it the passengers were fascinated and long-suffering, prepared to wait when Chris decided he wanted to take a shot of Simone in full ball-dress walking out of one of the tiny tunnels into the sunlight. Several were thrilled when Chris included them, signing the consent forms with an eager enthusiasm.

The afternoon venue was one of the stately homes up against the mountain, where Simone draped herself elegantly over the elegant Victorian furniture. All the time she felt Angus Grey's eyes on her, the full force of his personality bent on her in a single-minded concentration that made her uneasy. And yet, she thought some time during that busy, exhausting day, she didn't sense the taint of—what had it been, madness?—that had marred Jason's attitude towards her. In her innocence she had assumed that single-minded obsessiveness to be the intensity of genius. She had even, poor fool, been flattered by it.

But although Angus watched her with an absorption that sent secret chills across her exposed nerve-ends, he revealed only a patent, if reluctant, awareness.

Then it was over. They had worked quite literally from dawn to dark, and she was exhausted, as they all were. Foreseeing this, she had packed everything last night, and so was ready to catch the charter plane.

Chris approached her as she was going into her motel unit. 'You OK?'

She had given up battling the weariness that had lain in wait for her all day, and she wanted nothing more than to sleep, and to weep. 'I'm fine,' she said huskily.

'You did a good job today, a true professional. I was sorry to hear about your mother.'

She bit her lip and he slid an arm around her shoulder. 'I know what it's like,' he told her quietly. 'Sheer bloody hell. And there's nothing you can do about it.'

Grateful for his undemanding sympathy, liking him more than she had done until then, she leaned against him for a moment, borrowing a little of his strength. 'Yes, that's it,' she said gruffly.

'I'll see you back in Auckland.'

She managed to summon up a smile. 'I doubt it, unless we need to reshoot anything. I'm going away on holiday for a month. Good luck with the shots.'

'They'll get me the job I was looking for,' he said confidently, and lifted her face. 'Thanks, Simone.'

His kiss was pleasant, and he didn't attempt to deepen it, but neither was it a quick peck. When it was over he grinned and patted her backside in a gesture that was no doubt meant to be comforting. 'Keep your pecker up,' he said, and strode off into his unit.

A prickle of recognition pulled Simone's skin into tightness. Simone's head turned. Angus Grey was standing down where he and she had stood the night before. He had probably been gazing out over the untamed land but now he was looking directly at her. Sheer, undiluted menace radiated through the hot, dry air.

She smiled, a slow, sleepy, felinely taunting smile. Let him think what he liked, she thought, and lifted a hand in insolent greeting before going in.

A week later she sat on the bed in her motel room in Auckland, the first professional photograph she had ever sat for in her hands. The silver frame was cold, as cold as the grey day outside, and she was chilled through to the bone.

It was over. Her mother was buried, and she was entirely alone, except for an aunt her mother had quarrelled with before Simone was born. They hadn't communicated with each other since then. It was typical of Elizabeth Atkinson; her whole life had been a sorry tale of broken relationships and disappointment.

All her youth she had dreamed of the good life, resentful because with all her physical assets—the beauty she had cosseted and the elegant lines of her body—she had never got near it. Her job as assistant in a designer boutique had only whetted her appetite for the good things of life, leaving her more and more frustrated as the years went by. At last, swept off her feet by a physical passion that overwhelmed her in her mid-thirties, she had married a handsome, easygoing motor mechanic, who was never going to be anything else. He had been happy, and Simone had been happy, but her mother was not, torn by the twin devils of restlessness and discontent.

Until she had seen the advertisement for a modelling contest in one of the local magazines. Simone had just shot up from being a gawky child to a tall, slender adolescent, and her mother was the first to recognise her potential. Simone remembered it so well, that first photograph, and how the photographer had told her mother that the camera adored her.

God, she had been such a baby! She recalled her mother's elation when she'd won first prize, an appointment with the New York agent who had been making a talent-spotting foray into the South Pacific. At that interview Thea had been more than interested; she had been as excited as her imperturbable temperament allowed, offering Simone a contract then and there. Without a backward glance Elizabeth had packed and taken her daughter to New York, leaving behind her husband. He had died a year or so later, but not before Simone had become the newest sensation.

Elizabeth had loved it. At last she had realised all her dreams, living the life she had yearned for; she had had three wonderful years, until the disease that finally killed her had struck.

Simone shuddered. It had been hell. Elizabeth had refused to accept her condition until she was unable to function at all. In desperation, Simone had installed a nurse with her in the luxury apartment, but Elizabeth had hated the loneliness, continually demanding to go back to the country she had left with such alacrity.

So Simone was forced to bring her back home to New Zealand. By then a nursing home was the only viable alternative; Simone had hated to leave her there, but she'd had commitments to fulfil, and, as the money she had earned seemed to have slid through their fingers, she had to go back to work to pay for it all. Barely eighteen, she had been shattered at the loss of the only security she had—easy prey for Jason Sinclair, who'd told her he loved her, that he would look after her.

She had believed him. Jason was the flavour of the decade too, a brilliant painter from one of America's oldest families, a man who almost single-handedly had put the excitement and credibility back into representational art. Lean, good-looking in a dangerous blond fashion, he had burned with a ferocious fire. As fascinated as a moth by the candle's flame, when he had said that he loved her, that he wanted to marry her, Simone had been enraptured.

How green she had been! She had been violently in love with her handsome, charismatic husband. Almost

as much in love with him as he had been with her body.
Except that love didn't describe his emotions; Jason
worshipped her body, painting her in a variety of guises,
calling her his inspiration.

And she had been so young, so innocent, that she had
thought his obsession with her was love. Until they had
married.

Simone threw the photograph down on to the bed.
The knot of pain deep in her stomach tightened, making
her feel ill. She wanted to cry, but the tears wouldn't
come. Feeling old and tired and jaded, she lay back on
the bed and stared out into the garden, her eyes roving
from the cerise of the Judas-tree blossoms to the mauve
branches of the Genkwa daphne, graceful little har-
binger of spring. At its feet freesias bloomed; the scent
wafted in through the window, exquisite, chaste. Two
thrushes hopped across the lawn, and in the branches
of the Judas tree a tiny white-eye flipped and swung, its
olive-green plumage shining like burnished silk against
the white ring around its eyes and the sharp, shiny black
beak. The sun came out.

Simone pulled the eiderdown over her and wept herself
to sleep.

When she woke she rang through to her agent in New
York.

'Hi, honey, how are you?' Thea was her usual cheerful
self.

'Tired,' Simone admitted.

'Oh, you do need a holiday.' Thea's voice was absolutely certain. 'You've been working solidly for almost
a year. Take the whole month, Simone, and lie on a beach
somewhere in the sun. No, forget the sun. The pale look
is in this year. But rest is what you need. Your face is
not going to continue to earn us both a fortune if you
let it get tired and wan. And you don't have to be back
until the second of October.'

Simone sighed. 'It sounds wonderful,' she said quietly.
When she had hung up she surveyed her reflection with

the careful, impersonal professionalism she had achieved over the years. Thea was right: the glow was gone, the taunting, sensual laughter that was her trademark had faded completely. She looked her age, and she looked tired.

And it didn't do any good to tell herself that she was entitled to grieve; she had taken on work for the next year, and she had to fulfil her commitments.

But she needed rest, and peace. Not the artificial gaiety of a resort on a tropical island, or the busy socialising of a skiing holiday—tiredness was an ache in her bones. What she wanted was solitude, and a long beach where she could look for shells, and a garden in which to watch the spring arrive.

Two telephone calls later she knew exactly where she was going to stay.

Before she left she rang Julia at the magazine, and was greeted with effusive friendliness. 'Great to hear from you. How are things going?'

'Not too bad. I'm going up north for a while, so if you want to contact me you'll have to either ring me or drop me a postcard there.' She gave the address and telephone number.

'Right, got that. Where on earth is it?'

'Wainui Cove, north of Kerikeri. I've rented a bach there until the end of September.'

'Each to his own, I suppose; it'll be freezing at the beach this early in the season, but you enjoy yourself if that's your thing. I'm sure we won't need you, the proofs are fantastic. Chris excelled himself, and you are your usual superb self.'

'I'm glad.'

The next morning Simone flew to Kerikeri airport, picked up a hired car, and, after a glance at the map, wended her way northward through glowing green countryside where the farmhouse gardens were a blaze of colour from magnolia and camellia trees. Daffodils drifted in bold yellows across paddocks, sheltering lambs and calves as they lay in the sunlight. For once September was not living up to its reputation; although it was chilly, there was no wind and the sky was a clear, exquisite blue without a cloud in it.

Insensibly her heart lifted. In a way she had done her grieving for her mother before the poor woman had died. Those long years when Elizabeth had dwindled, until at the end she had been imprisoned in the shroud of her decaying mind, had been the years Simone had mourned. It was a horrible end to a life that had been a saga of wasted dreams.

Simone shivered under the impact of a vast loneliness. Her mother had been her one relative. She had wondered whether she should attempt to trace the woman who was her aunt, but somehow it seemed disloyal to Elizabeth's memory. Perhaps later, when the shock and the pain had receded a little.

A few miles north of Kerikeri she stopped at a general store and stocked up with groceries. There would be linen at the bach, but no food, although it possessed both a refrigerator and a deep-freeze. She bought basics and the fresh fruit and vegetables that the district was known for, received a warm smile from the woman behind the counter, and set off after checking the map once more.

The sun shone benignly down as she left the main road, turning right on to one that twisted and swooped between well-farmed hills, its verges dotted with wild peach trees in full pink blossom, until finally, after making her way carefully along a ridge set high above the sea, she crept down a hill so steep it was tar-sealed, to arrive at a long sweep of amber sand backed by a small settlement. To the south was a tree-covered headland, to the north a string of low islets that sheltered the bay.

With a soft sigh of relief she drove past the houses, some permanent residences, others obviously baches shut up for the winter. The gardens were gay with flowers, the houses could have come from any suburb in

Auckland. Around a hill at the far end of the settlement
a gate barred a farm-track.

Simone got out and opened it, standing for a moment
to look around. Ahead she could just see a small cove
bitten out of the much bigger bay. Great rounded domes
of pohutukawa trees lined the shore, backed by smoothly
swarded hills. Behind the little settlement the hills became
steeper, shaded blue-green by bush and second growth.
Apart from a couple of farmhouses nestled into trees,
she could see no buildings.

She breathed deeply, revelling in the crisp air, the salt
tang of the sea. Yes, this had been a good idea. Here
she would find healing and rest.

The drive across the paddocks was well-maintained,
but even so there were puddles, and the tracks of another
vehicle. The farmer, she assumed. After rounding another hill she came down on to the cove, sheltered by
the smooth contours of the hills from any winds, and
there, on a patch of grass above the small golden half-
moon of sand, sat the bach, low and unfussy and un-
pretentious—just what she expected.

When she got down she realised that it was actually
two units separated by two car-ports and a concrete block
wall. And unfortunately, the other one was occupied.

Simone stared resentfully at the offending Range
Rover, furious with the agent for not telling her, and
unreasonably angry with the people who were going to
share this corner of paradise with her.

Solitude had never seemed more desirable. But even
as she turned off the engine her usual placid good
humour was reasserting herself. Anyone who came here
at this time of the year was looking for peace just as she
was, so with any luck they needn't see each other at all.

And certainly there didn't seem to be anyone around.
No one came forth as she unpacked, there was no hint
or sign of anyone in the other little bach, exactly the
same as hers, with its big living-room, two double bed-

rooms separated by a spartan bathroom, and a washing machine and tub in a tiny room off the kitchen.

In spite of the sun the rooms were chilly and smelled slightly damp, so she lit a fire in the freestanding metal fireplace, glad to see an enormous pile of manuka logs in a corner of the car-port. While it caught she went outside to get her suitcase from the car; long years of travelling had taught her that, however fascinating the surroundings, it was always better to unpack before exploring.

Ten minutes later she was outside once more. Around the back a large Morrison's grapefruit tree bore golden globes of fruit; testing one for softness, she estimated they might be ripe enough to eat, although they were at their best later in the month. Next to it was a straggly Lisbon lemon. The pink buds and white flowers of jasmine clustered decoratively over a wire fence, through which was a paddock where two horses and a large brown and white goat grazed.

To one side was a flame tree, huge, bare except for the primitive, claw-like flowers. Simone tipped her head back, delighting in the flames licking against the pure sharp blue of the sky. Beneath it wild freesias bloomed; she picked a handful, sniffing their intense fragrance with delight, then a bunch of daffodils, freesias and sweetly scented jonquils. Once in drinking glasses, they gave that 'lived in' look, she decided as she made herself some lunch, a large sandwich of tomato and avocado and bean sprouts, and a cup of tea.

No one came to the other unit all that sunny, calm afternoon, and when she pulled the curtains that night there was no light in the sitting-room. Perhaps, she thought hopefully, that was where the Jacksons, the farming couple who owned the units, parked their own Range Rover. Although their house was up behind the hill, too far away for the unit car-port to be a convenient garage.

To her great astonishment, she slept soundly, not waking through the night as she had been since her mother's death. In the glowing, sunlit morning she lay for long minutes listening to the sound of small waves stroking the sand, and the cry of a seagull, harsh yet poignant. There was nowhere, she decided sleepily, nowhere she would rather be than right here.

And she was going to explore the beach right now. Yesterday she had been too tired to bother, but now vitality was running like rivulets of cool water through her. She pulled on jeans and an outsize shirt, slid her feet into sandshoes and snuggled into a big padded jacket in her favourite colour of deep peach, then slung a rusty woollen scarf around her neck, because although the sun was shining a chill little breeze was ruffling the quiet waters of the cove. And after the northern hemisphere summer she wasn't yet acclimatised to this crisp weather.

Receding waters had washed the amber sand so that Simone felt like the first person in a new, clean world. It took her about fifteen minutes to walk along the beach, stooping to examine shells, putting them all back except the absolutely perfect one that she had to keep.

When she reached the rocks at the end she scrambled up the hill, and making use of the narrow sheep-tracks, like contour lines on a map, walked around it until she reached the top. The grass was too wet to sit on so she leaned against a lichened old post, feasting her eyes on the panorama below. The trees on the hill to the south were outlined in gold by the sun, which had just risen above a band of cloud on the horizon, but the valleys were still in shadow. Before her the sea was softest dove-grey, shading to an exquisite pale blue. A band of burnished pewter stretched from the sun to the shore.

Entranced, she stood motionless until she sensed movements behind her.

She expected to see sheep, possibly the large red cattle with an exotic air to them that she knew to be Santa Gertrudis, but there was a man coming over the grass towards her, his long, powerful legs covering the ground in a lithe stride. A tiny prickle of unease pulled the skin over her backbone taut. She stared while the unease turned into full-blown shock. For it was Angus Grey.

Her mouth dried. Total amazement, underlaid with a frightening, unknown anticipation, stopped her from saying anything as he came up to her. Lord, but he was big! Her tilted green eyes searched the harsh austerity of his features, but they were totally uncommunicative. She didn't even know whether he had expected to meet her there.

'A far cry from Virginia City,' he said, smiling a little cynically at her frozen expression.

It took a lot to throw Simone, but this had done it. She had very carefully managed to banish him from her mind, and now his unexpected reappearance had breached those barriers, leaving her defenceless.

'Yes,' she replied huskily. She realised she was staring, and that he was amused by her astonishment, and she looked away, fixing her unseeing eyes on a small fishing-boat as it headed out towards the sun. 'Coincidence is an astonishing thing,' she said half beneath her breath.

There was a note of wry irony in the deep, crisp tones. 'Isn't it just?'

'When did you get here?'

'I drove up from Auckland yesterday.'

She nodded, pulling the woollen scarf away from her throat so that she could breathe more freely. 'I came yesterday, too.'

'I see.'

Yes, damn him, he was laughing at her! Temper spiked the words as she asked, 'Where are you staying?'

'In one of the units at Wainui Cove,' he said blandly.

Her stomach dropped. 'Well, coincidence upon co-incidence,' she said, swallowing hard. Why was she be-having like an idiot? Coincidence made fools of people time and time again; why should she be exempt?

He laughed, and she thought with involuntary appreciation that he had a very sexy laugh, although there was little warmth in it.

'I gather that's where you are, too,' he said. 'What decided you to come up here? It doesn't seem your sort of place. No cameras, no admiring crowds...'

'That's exactly why I'm here.' She managed to call up enough poise to hide the note of anger in her voice. There had been no overt nastiness in his tone; he had merely stated what he saw as a fact. And she had no intention of correcting him. She didn't care what Angus Grey thought of her.

'So even the camera's darling needs a rest from posing occasionally.'

She directed a scornful glance his way. 'Do you feel smug because most men would give their eye-teeth to be as tall and as well proportioned as you?' Without heat she let her eyes travel the length of his body in an assessment that was as impersonal as it was insulting, although she had to strive for that detachment, and her quickened pulse gave the game away.

That winged black brow climbed, but she couldn't see any emotion in the darkly aloof features. 'No,' he said with curt emphasis.

She nodded matter-of-factly. 'Neither am I proud of my looks, or that I photograph well. It's a matter of genetics. I'm glad that it's a marketable asset, but I've done nothing to earn it, so, like you with your height and build, pride doesn't enter into it.'

'I see,' he said neutrally. She had the feeling that she had surprised him.

'How long are you here for?' he continued when she made no attempt to speak again.

'Until the end of the month. You?'

'A few days beyond that.'

She said directly, 'You needn't fear that I'm going to disturb you. I'm here for peace and quiet.'

He laughed softly, his face conveying a vast cynicism. 'It's just as well, because that's all you'll be getting. It's a long way from the nearest disco.'

Angrily she swung to look up into that harshly angular face, searching for something that wasn't there. He was smiling, but it was an unsettling smile, as was the indigo intensity of his gaze.

'Good,' she said firmly, subduing the heat and flash of fury with some difficulty.

A gleam warmed the dense colour of his eyes.

Simone recognised it. Attraction. Desire. In some ways the basic building-block of human existence. Her wide shoulders moved fractionally. She turned away to shield her expression from that too-perceptive gaze, looking back out to the east and the joyous morning, not quite so joyous now that he was there, although her senses seemed to be honed to a greater acuity.

He said nothing, and she hurried away from such dangerous ground, asking, 'How are you getting on with your solar panels?' She stuffed suddenly chilly hands into her pockets.

'I'm not working on panels,' he said briskly. 'We'd better go; you look as though you're freezing.'

She walked beside him down the hill, keeping her eyes averted from the long, heavily muscled thighs beneath the corduroy of his trousers. Her skin felt cold, as though she had been too long in the wind, until she was suffused with a wave of heat. What is happening to me? she thought, striving to fight back the panic that threatened to overset her common sense.

'I thought you were trying to improve the panels,' she said, pushing her strange reactions to the back of her mind.

'No, the biggest disadvantage of solar power has been the difficulty of storing the power you make,' he told her. 'I'm trying to find some way to deal with it apart from storing it in batteries, which are bulky and inefficient.'

She was interested, and for the rest of the trek down the hill she managed to sublimate that blatant physical attraction by asking questions. Simone had not finished high school—she had been earning her living long before then—but she had regretted it and done her best to keep up by wide reading. However, she knew very little about the properties of electricity. Some of her questions must have sounded like the queries of an illiterate.

Surprisingly, for a man who apparently was close to being a genius, he wasn't irritated by her ignorance. In fact, he was amazingly patient, taking the time to explain carefully, so that by the time they reached the beach she had some idea of what he was trying to do.

Most men saw no further than her striking, gypsyish good looks and the slender sensuality of her body—most women, too, she admitted, inured to looks of envy and jealousy. Of the woman who lived within that exquisite shell, they knew little and cared less. It was intoxicating to be treated as a reasonable, intelligent human being.

'Would you like a cup of coffee, or tea?' she asked a little hesitantly when they reached the baches. Out at sea the sun-path had turned to molten gold and a little breeze was tugging at the long olive-green leaves of the flax bushes beside the units.

'Thank you. And I'll stop boring you with my work.'

'It's not boring,' she said shortly, pushing open the door. 'You make it interesting.'

Inside the sweet perfume of the freesias and jonquils blended with the warmth of the sun to make a combination that was purely spring. While Simone unwound the scarf from around her neck she said, 'Sit down, I'll put the kettle on. What would you like to drink?'

'Tea, thank you,' he said casually. As she walked into the kitchen he began to turn over the pile of books she had brought up to read.

She was pouring the water into the teapot when he said with the note of dry amusement she noticed so often in his voice, 'You really intend to holiday, don't you?'

Her deeply indented top lip straightened as she smiled, forgetting the effect that smile normally had on people. His eyes narrowed, but his answering smile was genuine.

Simone's heart did a funny double-thump in her breast. Oh, heavens, when he forgot to shelter behind the iron restraint he was altogether too much!

'Two big fat biographies, the history of an old scandal, three enormous romps, and——' he lifted his brow '—a very good, scholarly account of New Zealand's prehistory, which is going to take quite a bit of concentration.'

She shrugged. 'I know very little about it, and I am a New Zealander—I should know more.'

'I thought Julia referred to you as a citizen of the world.' The words were infused with irony.

Simone suddenly remembered going to Julia's unit the night that she had heard of her mother's death. Angus had been there, pouring drinks as though he belonged there. Had he stayed that night with Julia? A fierce, unexpected pang twisted her heart. She said briefly, 'It sounds good, doesn't it? But it doesn't mean anything.'

'A certain sophistication, surely?'

She shrugged. 'It depends how you define sophistication, I suppose. How is Julia?'

'Oh, she's fine, I believe. Thrilled with the results of the shoot.'

So he had been in contact with the fashion editor since they came home. But there was nothing to be gained from his tone. When it came to being non-committal Angus Grey could give diplomats points.

'Good,' she said inadequately, wondering why she should be so wretchedly conscious of the man who stood so much at ease in the room, watching her with those unreadable eyes. She knew what physical attraction was; what she had felt for her husband had been mainly that, the response of a very young woman to a sexy, exciting male. Which made what had happened afterwards so much more ironic!

But no other man had attracted her with this sort of consuming directness. It was like recognition, as though she and Angus Grey had been fated to meet, fated to want...

Fated to part, she thought as she asked him whether he liked milk or sugar. For there was no future for either of them in following up on this; it was a dead-end street.

No doubt, like so many men, he wouldn't be averse to a quick affair, no bones broken when it was over. If so he was doomed to disappointment. Simone had had bones broken and fingers burnt by her emotions, and she was not going to risk that pain again.

But he had talked to her as though she was just another human being, not the focus of men's fantasies and women's envy the world over.

Unknown to her, a small flicker of hope began to burn more brightly. She smiled at him, her glorious slanted eyes smoky and inviting, and handed him his tea. 'Tell me some more about solar power,' she invited.

An hour later she was still listening, enthralled. His enthusiasm forged life and colour in his conversation. Fascinated, Simone responded to the latent passion in every word. He made her laugh with his dry humour, and sigh as he detailed yet another failure.

'Shut me up,' he said calmly at last, although he had to know he wasn't boring her.

She said simply, 'Who said that genius is simply an infinite capacity for taking pains? I see now that he was right.'

'Carlyle. But he swiped the idea from a Frenchman, De Buffon, who said that genius is a great aptitude for patience. Whatever, both are important. But I'm not a genius, I'm an adaptor and improver and discoverer of unknown connections. Einstein was a genius.'

She didn't know enough about geniuses to argue with him, but she did say, 'Surely someone has to convert the theories to something useful?'

'There speaks the practical soul,' he said, smiling at her earnest face. 'A theory is like a symphony, or a poem; it doesn't have to be useful. It just is.'

It was a new idea to her, and one she pondered as she lifted tendrils of blazing hair back from her cheeks, annoyed with herself because she should have controlled her mane with a couple of combs as soon as she'd come inside.

But she hadn't been thinking straight. And she wasn't thinking straight now, either. For a moment she had almost suggested he stay to lunch. But if she invited him, he might think she was pursuing him.

He stood up in one smooth, powerful motion, graceful as an animal. 'I'd better be going,' he said. There was nothing in his strong face to indicate his thoughts. 'I'll see you around.'

'Yes. All right.' Her voice sounded stupidly breathless, and when he had gone she looked around the small, impersonal room with dazed eyes.

'Something's happening,' she announced out loud, but she smiled as she said it.

Of course, during the course of that sunny, silent day the euphoria faded so that by the time she was luxuriating in a bath before bed she was able to understand that she had only reacted to a man whose masculine charisma probably had the same effect on nearly every woman he came across.

OK, so he hadn't tried to rush her into bed, but he was a disciplined man; the will-power that controlled his needs and desires was written in the uncompromising contours of his face. And she, she thought with a vast determination, was just as strong. Ever since that doomed marriage she had been extremely wary of men, refusing to allow any to get close to her.

It hadn't been difficult; men who wanted her didn't seem to know what to do with the intelligent, thinking, feeling woman who lived inside the face and body of the decade, as she had been termed for too long now.

All they wanted was to sate themselves in the physical envelope, turn the laughing, challenging sensuality to their advantage, subjugate it with their own masculinity. She had been patronised by experts, by people who thought that a woman with a pretty face and good body couldn't possibly have any common sense or brains.

Even her mother, although she had loved her, had valued her for the money she earned, and the fact that she was able to live vicariously through her daughter. And not so vicariously; her mother had delighted in the good things money bought.

In her heart Simone longed to meet a man who understood that she was so much more than the glamorous creature who sold clothes and dreams. She had learned to tone down the teasingly provocative sensuality that was as much inborn as the brilliant hair and the slanted green temptation of her glance. Over the years she had constructed a mask that she removed only when she was in front of the camera, but, in spite of her coolness and detachment, men still pursued her for the wrong reasons.

So she knew herself to be particularly vulnerable to a man like Angus Grey, who made no secret of the fact that he was attracted to her, but who had the perception to see past the mask. Simone was accustomed to men who wanted her, but she could be seduced by his understanding, his acceptance of her lack of knowledge, and the fact that he didn't patronise her.

Especially as she felt that fierce tug of the senses too, the untamed summons that she was going to have to repress. Angus might be the most exciting man she had ever met, but she doubted very much whether he was in the market for marriage and children. And she had no intention of embarking on an affair with him.

There was something fiercely solitary about him, she mused, smoothing a handful of soap bubbles down one long, slender leg, something forbidden, unreachable.

But perhaps she was imagining things; it certainly seemed as though Julia was able to reach him! She leaped to her feet, swishing scented water from her slender ivory body, repressing the niggle of outrage that ached through her at the image of Angus kissing Julia, those broad shoulders shutting out the moon and the stars, the long, lonely nights...

CHAPTER THREE

'OH, FOR heaven's sake,' Simone scoffed, drying herself with quick, sharp strokes. 'You're becoming obsessed with the man!'

And while she drank tea and read from the fattest biography she put Angus Grey firmly from her mind.

Some time during the night a thunderstorm passed over, a dramatic orchestration of sound and light. Simone lay snuggled in her bed, listening to it with sleepy satisfaction, and fell asleep again to the sound of the rain that followed it.

It was still raining in the morning, so she added wood to the banked embers of the space heater and settled in for a long, glorious day of reading. Late in the afternoon the rain cleared, although the clouds still hung low around the hills. Restlessness drove her to pull on wet-weather gear, sling a pair of binoculars around her neck and set out along the beach. A long way ahead she saw Angus, like her, in anorak and gumboots, striding out across the hills. Her heart jumped, but she looked determinedly away down the beach.

The eternal movement of the tide had tossed up a fresh selection of pale shells and water-polished stones. Simone kept her head down, bending to pick up any that caught her fancy, standing with her back to the land for long moments while she stared out across the bay. The small creek at the side of the cove had brought down silt that stained a swath of putty-coloured murk across the water, marked with small, floating islets of branches and leaves.

One of these, an untidy bundle of debris held together only by the roots of the rushes that comprised it, was wallowing around on the edge of a current that would soon take it out to sea. Simone gave it a cursory look, then glanced back again, sure she had seen something moving there. She narrowed her eyes, looking slightly to one side to make use of her peripheral vision.

Yes, there was definitely something crouched between the rushes, but it was too small to see. After several seconds spent fiddling with the binoculars she got them focused on to the debris.

'A kitten!' she breathed, horrified as another wave took the makeshift raft further out. Kicking off her gumboots, she deposited her jacket and the binoculars on them, then ran down across the cold sand.

The bitter chill of the water made her gasp, but she set her jaw and strode further out. It was deeper than she thought, and the clump of debris was moving out to sea quite rapidly. As she struggled through the water the undertow snatched at her legs, tipping her slightly off balance. She managed to straighten up again, but the current was getting fiercer and the sodden little raft with its tiny, terrified passenger was being compelled further and further away from the shore.

She was up to her chest by the time she managed to grab the muddy leaves of the reeds. Waves slapped her arms and face, and she was so cold that she had stopped shivering and her body was one vast ache. The kitten, a tiny ginger and white, was spitting noiselessly at her, wet fur plastered against its tiny, thin form. its eyes, one deep amber, the other astoundingly cornflower-blue, blazing with fear and defiance.

'Oh, poor baby,' Simone muttered through stiff lips, trying to hold the leaves with fingers that felt thick and sausage-like. 'C-come on now, little thing, I'm only t-trying to help you.'

But to the kitten she was clearly the most horrific thing it had ever seen. Although no sound came forth its little mouth was stretched to its fullest extent, and when Simone reached out to lift it off the floating island it swiped her across the hand with razor-sharp claws, drawing blood.

Instinctively Simone leaped back and lost her footing, disappearing under the water. As she struggled back up, gasping and spitting in her turn, she almost panicked, for it seemed for one terrifying moment that her sluggish body was refusing to obey the commands of her brain. Which wasn't working too well, either. She couldn't think what to do next. But she forced her hand out to clutch the leaves once more, striving to keep the bundle out of the full force of the current.

At that same moment she heard Angus's voice, imperative, harsh with anger, call out something from behind.

'I won't b-be a m-minute,' she tried to call back, but she got another slap of water in the face, and the words were choked.

Suddenly she was in over her head, having to kick feebly to keep her face out of the icy clutch of the water, shivering so much that she couldn't get the kitten, still poised and ready to defend its life dearly, off. She clung on to the little raft, determined that after all this the little castaway would be saved.

It was no longer funny. Oddly enough, she wasn't afraid, for of course Angus would save her, but somewhere in her sluggish brain she understood she was going to have to get out of the water quickly or hypothermia could set in.

She couldn't turn around, but she heard him coming, recognising the swift, almost silent sound of his arms as they cut through the water.

He said nothing, merely clamped a hand under her chin and with the efficient power of a very strong man began to drag her back to the safety of the beach. Still with her hand clutching the floating island, Simone relaxed, her mind drifting into a pleasant numbness, until Angus stood up and hauled her to her feet, demanding harshly, 'What the hell do you think you're doing?'

So cold that she could barely articulate, she turned a pale face to him. 'It's a kitten, look, the p-poor little thing would have d-drowned.'

Swearing sensationally, he scooped the madly struggling kitten up by the scruff of its neck, hauled Simone upright, and calmed down enough to ask curtly, 'Can you walk?'

She staggered, but with his help she managed to make the few yards to the unit. By then she was shivering in real earnest, great, uncontrollable shudders racking her body. 'The k-kitten——'

He slammed the door behind them, dumped the struggling bundle of wet fur on to the floor, and lifted her up, carrying her effortlessly across to the bathroom. Once there he set the taps running and asked urgently, 'Can you get those clothes off?'

Although she tried, the wet jeans clung obstinately to her hips. Her hands wouldn't do what she told them. To her horror she discovered she was sniffing. 'They won't come off,' she muttered, dashing her tears away with a shaking hand.

She gave a muffled gasp, for Angus loomed through the steam like some primeval creature from a younger, more perilous earth, threatening, his hands outstretched.

'Right,' he said. 'Just relax, and do as I say. I have to get you out of those wet clothes.'

Before she could protest he pulled her jersey over her head and unbuttoned her shirt, pulling it swiftly away from her body and down her uncooperative arms. Then he unzipped her jeans and began to ease the wet material gently over her hips, his face absorbed yet impersonal. Simone shivered. Lethargy ran icily through her; she was almost able to ignore the primitive contrast of his dark, lean hands against the pale ivory of her skin, shielded only by white cotton briefs, the occasional brush of his sleek, wet hair on her chilled skin as he manoeuvred the garment down.

The denim was old and well-worn, so it hadn't chafed her, but it took quite some time for him to get the jeans down as far as her knees, and she got colder with each second that passed.

'Thank you,' she said, her teeth aching as she hugged herself. 'I can get them off from there.'

But he pushed them to her ankles. 'Step out,' he ordered in a harsh voice.

Shivering, looking down at the bronze head and impossibly broad shoulders, she stumbled out of the clothes.

'I'm all right,' she insisted.

He stood up with a single lithe movement, and looked down at her face. His own was impassive; there was nothing to give away his feelings, not even a glimmer in the darkly brilliant eyes. 'Can you get the rest off?' he asked.

She stepped back nervously, aware that her briefs and bra were probably almost transparent. 'Yes.'

'OK, hop into the bath. Don't stay in too long, or you could feel a bit faint. I don't think you've got hypothermia, but you'll need to warm up the core of your body, so keep your arms and legs out of the water. I'll make you some tea.'

'But what about you?'

'I wasn't wet nearly as long as you. I'm not even shivering.'

'You must be cold.'

He shrugged. 'I'll go next door and shower and change.'

She relaxed, but swung back as a new thought struck her. 'The kitten?' she asked almost pleadingly.

His mouth hardened. 'I'll deal with it.'

Shaken, her pulses running mad, she waited until he was out of the room before trying to wriggle out of the rest of her clothes. Her fingers were still clumsy, refusing to obey, so in the end, after a frustrated attempt to strip off her bra and pants, she struggled into the miraculously warm water of the bath with them still on, stretching her legs up the wall, making sure she kept her arms out. As ordered, she thought with a faint smile.

Dazed, her mind still numbed, she luxuriated in the exquisite sensations of returning warmth, but as soon as the shivering stopped and her heartbeat found its way back to normal she got out. Her bra and pants were still reluctant to leave her, but with circulation restored her hands were much more flexible now and she managed to haul them off before rubbing herself vigorously dry. Her dressing-gown was on the back of the door, thank heavens, so she slid into it, belting the warm green material tightly around her.

When she emerged, a little shy, Angus was swearing softly in the laundry. She forgot the unaccustomed shyness, forgot everything but the tiny castaway, and raced through to join him. Dripping wet and still spitting defiantly, the kitten was safely bundled up in a towel held in Angus's competent hands, while he dried it gently.

Simone stopped suddenly, her eyes fixed on his hands. 'Your hands!' she exclaimed.

He sent her an ironic look. 'It's a fighter. They'll be all right.'

'They don't look all right, they look as though you've been attacked by several bloodthirsty needles.'

He grinned. 'They'll recover. There, that's as much of the salt washed out of her as I can manage. I've put a hot-water bottle in this box, with a couple of towels. I suggest we put her here and give her some warm milk to drink, and with any luck she'll forgive us from rescuing her from a death by drowning.'

'Is it really a female?' She watched as he popped the pathetic little scrap into the high-sided box he had found from somewhere. He was firm with it, but gentle, and although the kitten registered disapproval it didn't seem quite so antagonistic as it had before.

'Yes, I checked.'

'Oh, that's a pity. I was going to call it Sinbad.'

He chuckled deeply. 'Why not?'

'I suppose there's no reason why not. Poor little scrap. How old is it, do you think? Is it big enough to leave its mother?'

'We'll have to hope so, won't we? I'd say it is; it looks six or so weeks old.'

She nodded, then said authoritatively, 'Those hands need seeing to. Come into the bathroom, I noticed a first-aid kit there.'

He had already showered and changed, and was now wearing well-cut trousers and a shirt in a soft greyed blue that somehow intensified the primitive purity of his incredible eyes. The cuffs were easy to roll up; Simone watched as his lean, beautiful hand deftly turned the material back.

After a moment she bit her lip and looked away to unscrew a tube of antiseptic cream. He held out an imperative hand, but she had already squeezed out a pearl of ointment, and without saying anything he let her smooth a small amount on to the long, oozing weals that the kitten had inflicted on him. Beneath her fingers his skin was smooth and hot, the hairs on the back of his hand soft yet wiry.

She saw her own long, slender, ivory fingers against the dark masculinity of his, and deep in the pit of her stomach something stirred.

'There,' she said quickly, unevenly, stepping back to put the tube of cream away. 'They should be fine now.'

'You're not going to put some sticking plaster on?'

She gave an enchanting gurgle of laughter. 'No, cuts are better left out in the fresh air. You'll be wanting me to kiss it better next.'

Now why on earth had she said that? But although he lifted an eyebrow he said merely, 'I think that only works with mothers.' His eyes sharpened as she went to put the cream away. 'The little devil got you, too. Here.'

His touch was oddly gentle, yet Simone felt it sear through her body, setting alight to nerves that had lain dormant for years. A swift, shaken second later she said huskily, 'Thanks.'

'Any time.' His tone was cool and composed. 'Come on, the tea's ready.'

She was ready for it, too. Without speaking, she turned away from him and went out into the sitting-room. 'Sit down,' he said as he poured the tea. 'Or, better still, lie down on one of those divans.'

She shrugged, but tiredness seemed to have drained the stuffing from her bones, and she obeyed, arranging her gown to cover her legs after she curled up on the divan. He put the cup of tea on to the small table and sat down opposite her, a mug held in his competent hand.

'Thank you for coming to my rescue,' she said, afraid for some reason of the silence. 'I was getting a bit worried out there.'

He lifted that speaking eyebrow. 'I suppose it's no use telling you that it's stupid to risk your life for an animal, however small?'

'I'm not silly,' she asserted, frowning a little as she met his eyes. 'I honestly didn't think I'd have any difficulty at all. It wasn't far off the beach.'

'And the tide was coming in, and the harbour is awash with the run-off from last night's rain,' he said sarcastically. 'Common sense should have told you to at least make sure that someone else was around before you started rescuing things. Promise me you won't do anything like that again.'

She nodded, because of course he was right, she had been reckless.

'Would you like to have dinner here?' she asked a little shyly—she who had long ago given up being shy! 'It's the least I can do, as you came to both our rescues!'

'Can you cook?' She bristled, and he laughed, for once without the deep-seated mockery that normally hardened both his smile and his laughter. 'It doesn't matter, because you're in no state to try. Incipient hypothermia is not something to be tossed off lightly. However, if you promise not to give me advice, I'll get what I was planning to have and bring it over.'

She arched her perfect brows at him. 'You can cook?'

'Bachelors,' he told her kindly, 'learn to cook, or they starve. My mother has very firm ideas on equality between the sexes. My sister knows her way around an engine, and I'm not a bad cook, although my repertoire tends to consist of dinners that can be prepared and cooked in half an hour.'

She said quietly, 'You have a mother. You're lucky.'

The planed angles of his face seemed to harden, if that was possible, but he said politely, 'I was sorry to hear that yours had died.'

'In lots of ways it was a blessing,' she replied, keeping her lashes down so that he couldn't see her emotions. The last thing she wanted to do was burst into tears in front of him. Instinct told her that any sign of weakness would put her at a disadvantage.

'She'd been ill before she died?'

She nodded. There was a moment's pause, a watchful, waiting tension that made her say too quickly, 'And you have a sister too. You're lucky. I was an only child.'

'Yes,' he said, with a faint but perceptible withdrawal.

Outside the rain drummed down, enclosing them in their little cocoon of light and warmth. Did it ever rain like this in Virginia City? Judging by the sparse vegetation on the hills around, it seemed highly unlikely. And certainly no waves washed near there as they did here, pounding heavily on to the amber sand in spite of the shelter of the hills and the harbour.

So his family was off-limits! With an effort she ignored the ache of loneliness his rebuff had caused, and drank the rest of the tea, setting the mug down on the table he had pulled up beside the divan. He looked across to where she lay, her long body gracefully disposed, hair like a pool of fire around her seductive, sultry face. Simone felt that look right down to her toes. A hot shudder swept through every cell, emerging as goose-bumps on her skin.

He gave her a smooth, thin smile and began to talk of the latest film sensation.

Simone followed his lead, ignoring the turmoil in her bloodstream. She didn't care what Angus Grey thought of her, she told herself as their conversation moved on to the latest sensational novel. She really wasn't interested in him. But honesty forced her to admit the truth; she was, but self-preservation indicated that she make sure her emotions never got beyond interest. He was too much for her to handle.

A movement at the base of the bench that separated the kitchen from the living-room caught her attention. 'I think,' she said softly, 'that Sinbad has discovered a way to get out of the box.'

Sure enough, the marmalade kitten was peering around at them, its mismatched eyes wide and wary. Dry, its little stomach rounded by the milk, it looked a far cry from the bedraggled castaway they had rescued. Slowly Angus turned his head. The kitten surveyed him with silent caution.

'Oh, it's so sweet,' Simone breathed. 'Four white paws and a white neck-cloth.'

'Sweet is not exactly the term I'd use to describe it,' Angus said, adding drily, 'It's a warrior, an Amazon.'

Simone gave a gurgle of laughter. Immediately Sinbad disappeared behind the counter, but after a few silent seconds peeked suspiciously around again.

'Don't look at it,' Angus advised. 'Just let it wander around.'

'Shouldn't we butter its paws so it won't run away? And what about a dirt box?'

'It's there,' he said. 'I put some sand in another box. Cats are clean animals so with any luck it'll be house-trained. And if you keep it inside for a couple of days it will associate food with you, and won't try to run away. But you may have some difficulty taming it. Its mother was a wildcat, and this little one will be wild for some time.'

They continued talking and, sure enough, the little warrior ventured a few steps into the room, although when Angus got to his feet to put some more wood on the fire it disappeared once more.

'I'll get that food,' he said as he stood dusting down his lean, strong hands.

Simone nodded, warm and oddly lazy, her body tingling with unknown sensations. The rain had eased, although it was still coming down heavily enough to make her glad she wasn't out in it; but here she felt safe, oddly protected, no longer alone. 'Is there anything I can do?'

'Stay right there.'

When he had gone the impersonal room seemed suddenly colder, and much bigger. Of course he was a big man, but he seemed to take up a lot of space. Psychological space, she thought. He didn't allow people to get close to him.

An image of Julia's elegant, sophisticated face swam into her mind, and she wondered again just how close they were. Sighing, she closed her eyes. It was none of her business. If he and Julia were lovers—well, good luck to them, although the fashion editor had to be at least four years older than he was.

Simone was dozing when he arrived back. She lifted her heavy lashes, realised that it was him, and sent him a sleepy smile of great sweetness as she lifted her torso on to an elbow prior to getting up.

'Stay where you are,' he ordered, his voice harsh enough to banish the smile.

She lay watching him move around the kitchen, her nose wrinkling with the savoury odours that came wafting out in a very short time. Beef stew, she decided, listening to her stomach rumble. And jolly good stew it smelled, too. Clearly he wasn't boasting when he said he could cook. What were his mother and his sister like?

Did they too have that disturbing intensity, controlled by such fierce discipline?

It was—frightening, yet powerfully attractive. What would Angus be like as a lover? Did he still hold his emotions under such ferocious restraint, or did he let them slip loose? How would it feel to be the woman on whom that intensity was focused? A shiver of sensation ran from deep in her stomach when her mind conjured up the memory of his sleek bronze head brushing against the wet, sensitive skin of her thighs while he yanked her jeans down, his hands dark against her skin, strong, yet gentle...

Arousal surged through her in a hot, sweet, debilitating flood. Appalled, she banished the exciting images from her brain, and tried to impose some sort of cold logic over the singing desire that held her in thrall. It was just passion, just the need of a woman for a man. She was twenty-five, and her body-clock was telling her it was time she was bedded and given a child, and Angus Grey was the most potent male she had seen for a long time.

But rationalise it as she might, it wouldn't go away. Unwilling to admit that she wanted to know much more about this intriguing man, so aloof, yet so good at taking care of a woman, she fixed her eyes on to the flames in the fireplace; but her peripheral vision, in many ways much more acute than forward vision, registered the lithe masculine grace of his movements, the lean male triangle of shoulders and hips, the tight buttocks, the long strength of arms and legs.

Oh, God, she thought feverishly, staring into the flames that seemed pale and listless compared to the inferno that raged through her. Oh, God, this is lust, and, if I weren't experienced enough to know that lust is nothing, it is less than nothing without the right feelings, I'd be in his bed tonight.

'I brought some wine over, but I don't think it would be a good idea,' he said, startling her.

Why not? Because it might loosen even more of her inhibitions? Unwelcome colour heated the length of her cheekbones, made the skin on her neck and breasts prickly and uncomfortable.

'The one thing you must not give hypothermia patients is alcohol,' he finished.

She nodded, touching parched lips with her tongue, swallowing before she could say in a fairly steady voice, 'There's no reason why you shouldn't have some, though.'

'No,' he said, coming back into the room. 'I don't drink alone.'

It was on a par with what she knew of him, that formidable authority that set a barrier between him and the rest of the world, except, perhaps, his family.

He came to stand beside her, looking down at her with a faint frown between those straight, winged brows. 'How are you feeling?'

'A little tired, but I think that's probably the fire,' she answered honestly, thankful that she was able to hide the untamed sensations that rioted through her.

'Possibly, but hypothermia can be tricky.'

She frowned. 'Angus, I was only in the water for fifteen minutes or so.'

'And from the first symptoms to unconsciousness need take only forty minutes,' he said grimly. 'Especially in cold water.'

The colour slowly bleached from her face. 'I didn't know that.'

'No, too many people have no idea of the symptoms, or that they can get it so easily and quickly.'

Shadows darkened the pale jade of her eyes. She shivered a little, realising anew how foolish she had been. Averting her head from that intent scrutiny, she confessed sheepishly, 'I'm very thankful you were there. I was getting a bit panicky until I heard you call.'

She looked up into eyes as turbulent as molten sapphires, but instantly the thick, curly lashes dropped. 'I know,' he said in the detached voice that seemed so at odds with the smouldering embers of his eyes. 'Be more careful in future.'

'Oh, I will.' Her fervour was quite unfeigned, and he smiled obliquely and left her, pulses fluttering like the wings of a captured bird, because his smile slid straight through her defences and lodged in her heart.

He let her sit at the small chrome and Formica table while she ate dinner, but when the last delicious mouthful had gone, he said, 'Back on to the divan while I wash the dishes.'

'No,' she said firmly. 'I'll do them in the morning. The cook never washes the dishes.'

He sent her a quizzical look. 'This one does. Go on, back on to the divan.'

She opened her mouth but met his gaze, implacable, cool, and closed it again. He looked as though he'd have no compunction about picking her up and depositing her on the divan, and she did not want that.

'You are incredibly bossy,' she grumbled as she got to her feet. 'I'll bet you were a tough older brother.'

He grinned. 'Yes.'

'And she still speaks to you?'

'She does,' he said, something extinguishing the amusement as though a shutter had come down.

Disposing her long limbs on the divan, Simone wondered what had caused that withdrawal. Perhaps he and his sister had been estranged for a while. Another shiver, but this time a cold one, touched lightly on her nerve-ends. She wouldn't like to get on his wrong side; instinct warned her that he wasn't a man who found forgiveness easy.

He left as soon as he'd washed and dried the dishes, after building up the fire in the space heater and telling her that he'd be back in the morning. On a soundless sigh that had to be relief, Simone locked the door behind him.

Exciting he definitely was, intriguing, even fascinating, but he was exhausting too. When he was anywhere near her she felt too much, emotions and sensations blended into an unholy alliance that kept her on edge.

Smiling rather ironically, Simone peeped in through the laundry door. Sinbad had found her way back into the box Angus had prepared for her, and was asleep, although she bristled and spat when Simone turned the light on. Apparently she was house-trained. The dirt-box had been used.

'Sleep well,' Simone said softly and withdrew to her bedroom.

As she brushed her hair she looked at her reflection in the mirror. Her face looked back, just the same as it had always been. It was odd that a virgin should have a face that promised all sorts of sensual delights, but that was the fault of her full mouth and slanted green eyes, and the high cheekbones that gave her an exotic, smouldering look. Oh, she was versatile, she could look innocent, even wistful when it was required, but the wilful, laughing sensuality was always there, so that it was an unawakened houri who beckoned from the pages of magazines.

It was a mask, the face the world knew. Just as much a mask as the impassive features that formed the framework of Angus's countenance, clamping in his emotions and his thoughts, so that he was impossible to read clearly. What had happened to make him like that?

On this thought she drifted off to sleep and, whether it was the hypothermia or just exhaustion, she slept solidly until something alien woke her. For a second she didn't know where she was and lay rigid, trying to establish her whereabouts. Of course, the bach at Wainui Cove. She lay listening. The rain had stopped, and all she could hear was the sound of the waves on the beach, not as noisy as they had been, she noted. So what had woken her?

She turned over, and looked about her in the dim, early morning light that seeped through the curtains. And there, on the other side of the big double bed, was Sinbad, curled up almost under the eiderdown, sound asleep.

Simone chuckled noiselessly. How had the little thing got up this far? Had she been lonely for her littermates, drawn towards the only other living being in the bach for comfort?

Still smiling, she drifted back to sleep.

The sun trying to get in through the curtains woke her again. Simone lay quietly, watching the kitten clean itself with impassioned fervour, and then, after tentative looks, begin to pat at a lock of hair that had floated across to its side of the bed.

Repressing her laughter, Simone realised that it was going to be difficult to give up this delectable little thing when she went back to work. She would have to find it a good home, she promised herself, a home where its fey, elfin charm was appreciated. She had never seen a cat with eyes of different colours before, and such pretty colours.

A knock on the door brought her upright. It was seven-thirty, but she was on holiday, after all! Clearly Angus was an early riser.

'OK,' she called, scrambling out and into her dressing-gown. Barefooted, her hair rioting around her, she ran across to the door, a beatific smile tugging at her mouth.

He was leaning against the post, looking out to sea. As Simone opened the door he straightened up, turning to meet her radiant smile with lifted brows. 'Good morning,' he drawled. 'I can see I don't need to ask how you are.'

She laughed. 'No, I'm fine. Isn't it a fabulous day? Like something out of the dawn of time, all fresh and new and sparkling.'

His eyes moved past her to the floor. That hard mouth quirked. 'I see you've won over your small sailor,' he remarked.

Simone laughed softly as she watched Sinbad playing with the girdle of her gown, batting it with a small white paw, her tail swishing around.

'She climbed into my bed during the night,' she said. 'I suppose she was lonely.'

'I suppose she was.' Something had altered in his smile, so that there was less humour in it, perhaps a touch of cynicism. The intense blueness of his gaze scorched through her.

'You have amazing eyes,' she blurted.

'So have you.'

What is the matter with me? Her brain seemed to have seized completely; she even felt dizzy. 'Mine are shallow,' she said dismissively, speaking objectively as she always did when it came to her looks. 'But yours are so dense with colour! Pure lapis lazuli. I don't think I've ever seen eyes that colour. If you were a woman—or another man—I'd suspect that you were wearing coloured contact lenses. And those lashes are positively indecent for a man.'

Faint colour stroked along the high, stark cheek-bones. 'I suppose I'm flattered. I was born with these eyes, so my mother tells me. And in spite of your disclaimer, you must be aware of the power of those green eyes. As pure in colour as the best jade, limpid and seductive, eyes that stay in a man's mind.'

Simone blinked. Had they stayed in his? She managed to summon up a smile, and say casually, 'Thank you, but green eyes are quite common.'

'So are blue,' he said, equally casually. 'I'm going in to Kerikeri today, do you want to come?'

There was nothing she needed, but she found herself saying, 'Yes, I'd love to come, thanks.'

Two hours later she was sitting beside him in the large, very luxurious Range Rover, eyeing the countryside with interest as they moved down the road. Obviously accustomed to gravel back-country roads, Angus drove skilfully, and after five minutes she relaxed, content to put her safety in those lean, competent hands and his quick reactions.

The sun beat in the window, easing her tension. If it were possible, she thought with a bubble of laughter that was somehow a part of the glittering day and the heady sense of excitement, she would purr!

'That's a small, smug smile,' he said, adding with an uncanny echo of her own thoughts, 'Almost feline.'

'I was just feeling lazy and pampered, like Sinbad. I'm going to get a cat box while we're in town and I'll make an appointment for her to see the vet as soon as possible. She'll need to be immunised, and I want her checked over properly.'

'You'd better take some gloves,' he advised drily. 'You haven't tamed her yet, you know. And it would be a pity to add more scratches to those soft hands.'

'How are yours?' She was shaken. She had been so delighted with the day and his presence that she had forgotten to ask. Leaning forward, she tried to see.

'Fine.' He extended one. 'Almost better.'

His hand accidentally caught the soft curve of her breast. Simone felt a dart of sensation, sharp as a spear, all the way through her. She dragged in a sudden breath, and he said coolly, 'Sorry,' and slid his hand back on to the wheel again.

Simone didn't say anything; she couldn't, she was too busy trying to banish the searing delight of that gentle, accidental touch.

She had never felt anything like it before. Even with Jason, whom she had thought she loved—heaven help them both—it had never been like this. She didn't want to feel these things with Angus Grey. She didn't want to start on that path again. Her marriage to Jason had been doomed—a nightmare that left her severely scarred. A relationship with Angus would be just as ill-fated.

So she would have to pretend that she saw him just as an interesting, rather forbidding man, not one who made her blood sing through her veins.

'You're frowning now,' he said calmly. 'What's the matter?'

'Nothing. There's something I wanted to buy,' she improvised, 'and I can't remember what it is. Oh, look! Isn't that lovely?'

The road dived down through a small gully and across a bridge, and beside the creek were several kowhai trees, their graceful, drooping branches studded with yellow, parrot-beaked blossoms. Against the dark olive-green of the small patch of trees behind them they glowed like sunlight rendered into substance, elegant, beautiful, and only ever to be seen in New Zealand.

'Yes,' he said, and brought the vehicle to a halt. 'Let's get a closer look.'

She was wearing toast-coloured corduroys and solid shoes below her cashmere jersey and heavy jacket, so she had no hesitation in jumping out and following him down the steepish bank. The sound of water running over the stones blocked out any noise. Almost immediately the resident fantail came fluttering around them, its beady black eyes and small body alert and distinctive as it caught the tiny unseen insects their progress roused.

The creek chattered shallowly over a series of basins carved in the dark rock; there was cushiony moss, ferns in a variety of forms, and the indescribable freshness of the bush and the water. The scent of honey teased her nostrils; she leaned over and sniffed, finally tracking it down to the delicate greenish flowers of one of the scrambling bushes beneath the kowhai trees. Simone looked around, a little smile touching her mouth.

'If your tame photographer were here now he'd take a picture and call it the spirit of Northland,' Angus drawled.

Simone covered her uneasiness by looking comically down at her solid shoes. 'A very substantial spirit.'

Jason had painted a picture of her lying naked in a bed of ferns, and called it *Spirit of Desire*. She had hated it, but he had promised her that it would never be sold—and she had hoped that the blatantly sexual pose might help whatever it was that he suffered from, the block that prevented him from consummating their marriage.

CHAPTER FOUR

IT HADN'T; nothing had helped, Simone thought bitterly. Jason had worshipped her body with a fervour that came close to fanaticism, but for the five months of their marriage he had refused to make love to her. He had used his brushes and his paints to idolise her, but he had believed with a superstitious fervour that if she lost that tantalising mixture of seduction and innocence he wouldn't be able to paint her again. 'Anticipation makes love sweeter,' he had said.

He had been wrong.

At least the paintings had been destroyed. His agent had been horrified when she'd insisted on that after Jason's death, almost weeping as he told her they were the best things Jason had ever done, accusing her of being a Philistine; but she had been adamant, and in the end all the nudes Jason had painted during the painful months of their marriage had been burnt.

Thank God. She had hated posing for them, and hated the results. There had been something—wicked, about them, something heated and unhealthy that still had the power to make her skin crawl.

'You could never be sturdy,' Angus commented, surveying her with open appreciation. 'Even in those clothes you look like a thoroughbred.'

'Thank you,' she said simply, unexpectedly confused by the casual compliment.

He smiled. 'I mean it.'

That unexpected shyness returned as she looked up. He was standing in the shade of the trees, tall and dark and...*still*, as though he was waiting for something. Confused, she turned away, because that watchful waiting made her more than uneasy—it made her very wary. Yet when he strolled out into the sunlight he looked the same as he usually did, no sign of a threat unless it was that of his unleashed masculinity.

You're imagining things, she scoffed.

It was the school holidays, so Kerikeri was bustling with people, both tourists and locals. Simone was accustomed to being stared at, but New Zealanders tended to be more tactful in their admiration than many other nationalities, and although she was aware of the interest she was causing she was not bothered by it.

'I feel like a celebrity,' Angus said, a subtle irony shading his voice.

Simone sent him a sly, sideways glance. 'Oh, yes? I'm not in the least surprised, with the avid looks you've been getting from every woman.'

He looked a little taken aback, and then displeased, as though he didn't like to think of himself as an object of interest.

'That's because I stand head and shoulders above most other men,' he said curtly.

Simone chuckled. 'Is that it? I can assure you that although the men might be admiring your height the women are not. Or not entirely.'

Something glittered in the dark eyes as his gaze swept her face, deliberately pausing on her mouth and the slender ivory length of her throat. 'Do you admire my height, Simone?' he murmured.

She fluttered her lashes at him, exhilarated by the light flirtation. This she could deal with; in fact, she was an expert at it. 'Of course. We go together well, don't we? There aren't all that many men around who are taller than I am.'

He grinned. 'Or women who don't make me feel like a clumsy giant.'

'Clumsy?' Her brows rose as she looked him over, paying him back for the slow survey of a minute ago. After a moment she said drily, 'I find it difficult to imagine that you ever feel clumsy.'

He looked amused, but didn't reply, and, after buying the cat basket and making an appointment for Sinbad, they set off home again. A few minutes along the road he asked, 'Do you like picnics?'

'Love them.'

'I bought some food, and I happen to know a good place that's crying out for a picnic.'

He turned off on to another gravel road, but this one went inland through some of the citrus and kiwifruit orchards that were such a feature of the landscape around Kerikeri, and then on through farmland, climbing all the way.

After a few miles he said, 'Look through the back window.'

And there, spread like a tapestry below them, was land behind the Bay of Islands, from the farms and orchards with their huge shelterbelts of eucalypts around Kerikeri to the two heads—Purerua, volcanic and craggy in the north, and stark Cape Brett with Piercy Island guarding the southern entrance.

'Oh, that's beautiful,' Simone said on a long, satisfied sigh.

He turned into a gateway and drove over a cattlestop and down a long metalled road through rich paddocks where sleek Black Angus cattle grazed, their delightful calves rollicking around them in the warm sun.

'Isn't this trespassing? Won't we get thrown off the property by an irritated landowner?' Simone asked a little nervously.

'No, I know the owner.'

She nodded, settling down to watch the shifting contours of the scene below, speckled with purple cloud shadows, the blue, blue waters of the fretted Bay a dazzling contrast to the hills and valleys and little plains. It reminded her of the landscapes Italian painters of the Renaissance used as a background to their portraits— remote, blue-hazed, a small peep-hole into fairy country.

Angus stopped the Rover in a little cup of the hills that sheltered them from the slight wind. For a moment after the engine died he sat surveying the scene and looked out over the green paddocks in front of them with a slight, satisfied smile. Neither speaking, they shared a communion that had nothing sexual in it—merely the comfortable companionship of friends.

The smile deepened, creasing into his lean cheek, and awareness sizzled through Simone. His eyes narrowed but he said merely, 'Let's see what we've got, shall we? We'll have to eat out of the car as it's too wet to sit down, but if you don't mind that...?'

'No,' she said, shaken, 'I don't mind.'

Mind? At that particular moment she wouldn't have minded anything!

He had bought delicious chilli mussels from the delicatessen, a pâté that blended with slices of avocado to form ambrosia, crisp French bread and crackers, and chicken legs studded with sesame seeds in a rich oriental marinade, as well as tomatoes, and, to finish, delicious little mandarins like glowing orange jewels. There were also two bottles of mineral water.

Had he remembered how much she liked this particular brand? Or was it just a coincidence?

'Don't you like the pâté? You don't have to eat it,' he said.

She laughed and shook her head. 'No, the food's delicious. I was—thinking of something else.'

'Something unpleasant, I gather.'

Her wide shoulders lifted momentarily. 'No, not at all.' Her tone made it clear that she wasn't going to expand.

He lifted his brows but said nothing. The sun shone on to the chiselled angles of his face, emphasising the autocratic framework, the stark, hard contours. Simone watched covertly as he demolished a chicken leg, wondering what those strong white teeth would feel like...

Stop it! she ordered her wayward and altogether too creative mind. Stop it this instant!

A skylark launched itself into the sky, pouring out a flood of lyrical notes. Something light and hopeful expanded in Simone's breast, tingling through her body to emerge as a radiant smile while she searched out the tiny dot that was the passionate songster.

Angus waited until the end of the outburst of joy, then offered her a paper napkin. 'Have I got a crumb on my face?' she asked, the incredible access of delight making her less cautious than usual.

He looked at her mouth with half-closed eyes, and smiled too. 'Yes,' he said, bending. 'Just—there.'

The crumb was beside her mouth; he flicked it free with his thumb and then bent his head a little further and kissed her, lightly, the merest touch of firm, cool lips.

Sensation beat suffocatingly high in her throat. Her lashes fluttered down, so that the last thing she saw was the brilliant blue glitter of his eyes. And then he kissed her properly.

It was like being touched by a god, she thought dazedly, painful yet dazzlingly exciting. His mouth was imperious, confident, as though he was fully in control of his actions, but she was lost within a few seconds, listening with astonishment to the thunder of her heartbeats in her ears. The world began to slide away from beneath her feet. Unconsciously her hands clenched on to his shirt, and through the material she could feel the heat of his body sear her palms.

'You kiss like a child,' he said, amusement sweetening the insult. 'Open your laughing mouth, Simone, sweet...'

She stiffened slightly. Jason used to kiss her like that—deep, deep kisses that stirred her blood and set her gasping; but they had left her frustrated and angry when he had refused to follow through.

'Open for me,' Angus ordered, his voice deep and hypnotic, adding with the faintest of laughs, 'I promise I'll respect you afterwards.'

And the memory of Jason slipped into the past where it belonged, no longer able to hurt. Jason had never been able to laugh at himself or her.

Simone allowed Angus to part her lips, still taut, still holding herself stiff, but he was gentle, his tongue touching only the insides of her lips, tracing the sharp serrations of her teeth with subtle, diabolical insight. She sighed, and his arms contracted, holding her warmly against his big body, protecting her from the wind, from anything that might harm her.

Fire leapt through her, and she yielded to its demands. He must have sensed her surrender, for his mouth hardened, demanded instead of coaxed, and in an instant she was enveloped in a conflagration of desire.

It was like nothing she had ever experienced before. This was why she had been so wary, yet now, when she was locked in his arms, her body straining against his, she knew she had no reason to fear him.

Sensation pooled in the pit of her stomach, ached in her breasts, calling for her complete surrender. He took what he wanted with the fierce pride of a conqueror, subduing her so that her world narrowed down to this, the heat of the sun on her back and the strong body of this man against her, compelling, insisting that she accept his dominant, seeking mouth.

But she was no submissive woman, acceptant, meekly taking what he offered. She returned his kiss, her hands suddenly fierce around his back, the palms tingling as she felt the muscles bulge and coil when he leaned back against the vehicle.

Mindless, helpless, she reacted without volition to the pulsating energy of his need, half lying against him so that the fact that he was aroused was completely obvious. She didn't care. She was aroused too, aching for the fulfilment her instincts knew he would be able to give her. Generations of women in her ancestry nodded and smiled secret smiles, and whispered how to arch her body, offering everything she had to him, all that was Simone Atkinson.

He lifted his head. She opened dazed, slumbrous eyes, staring at the harsh features of his face, drawn stark with a primal need, and the wide mouth that had given her such ecstasy.

'God,' he said unevenly, a pulse throbbing in the bronzed column of his throat.

Simone's lashes dropped. She put her mouth to the hidden messenger, feeling his life beating unsteadily beneath her lips.

His big body jerked as though she had hit him in the solar plexus. 'Simone,' he said harshly, and kissed her again, on the pure ivory line of her throat, on the tender place where her jawbone hinged, and then forward to her earlobes and the soft, erotic place beneath them—little biting kisses that stung yet sent her passion rocketing further and further.

And then, when she was so taut with tension that she couldn't speak, couldn't do anything but sigh and lift her face in mute request for more, he put her to one side and said harshly, 'We'd better go home.'

Familiar frustration exploded inside her, eating away at her composure—a sly, seeping black confusion worse than it had been six years ago, leaving her smirched and angry.

She looked up into his face, her own white with emotion, and saw that he was adamant. Gone was the hungry lover of a moment ago; his iron will had pulled a mask down over his features, and even his eyes were blank, almost black beneath those long, curling lashes.

Slowly her hands dropped from around him; she stepped back, chilled to the bone, aware for the first time that her mouth was burning with the impact of his kisses.

Yet it was not his fault; as she took several deep breaths common sense took over, banishing the mists of passion, and with it came shame. She had been a more than willing partner in those kisses.

'Yes,' she said emptily.

Without further speech they packed up, taking care not to touch each other, and left the sunny little dimple in the fold of the hills. The sun shone just as brightly, but somehow the glorious day had become brassy and obvious. As the ache of unfulfilled desire faded Simone was faced with another driving emotion—humiliation.

How could she have pressed herself against a man she had known for such a short time and do everything but ask that he take her? She sneaked a look at his profile, etched with the arrogant clarity of a silhouette against the green, smiling countryside. He looked severe, the wide mouth held well under control, the softening effect of the cleft in his chin lost from that angle.

He turned and caught her survey. Something leapt in his eyes, and his mouth curled. 'Don't look so shattered,' he said calmly.

Colour surged up from her throat. 'I am shattered.' Her voice was husky. 'I don't normally—I mean, I don't——'

The hard twist of his mouth eased into a scarcely less hard smile. 'Neither do I,' he told her.

Did that mean that he hadn't spent the night with Julia in Virginia City? Probably; certainly the day following had not been marked by Julia's sated pleasure. She had been just the same as she always was, perhaps even a little acerbic.

Simone shuddered. If she had spent the night in Angus's bed neither he nor she would look the same. Something powerful and fierce, as elemental as the shape of the hills and the sea, had leapt full-grown into life when they had kissed, and however much she might regret its genesis it was too late to contain it now. The only way to control it was to refuse it any further licence.

She sat back in her seat, keeping her gaze firmly on the road ahead. It didn't matter whether or not he had made love to Julia or any other woman, because he wasn't going to make love to Simone Atkinson. All of her forebodings had been more than accurate; he was dynamite, dangerous and terrifyingly attractive to her, and she wasn't going to be able to fight him off if she allowed more of those deep, drugging kisses.

Firmly repressing a ripple of recollection along her nerves, she frowned. So that was it. No more.

The rest of the drive home passed in taut silence. Back at the cove she thanked him formally for the ride and the lunch, the cat basket she had bought at the vet's clutched firmly in her hand.

He surveyed her aloof face with a narrowed, sardonic gaze. 'I'll see you around, then,' he said, and, as if to underline what had happened, bent his head and kissed her cheek.

Speechless, Simone watched him stride back to his bach, her hand absently rubbing the hot skin while she adjured her quivering nerves to calm down. The sun struck bronze sparks from his head; he walked easily, confidently, his height and bearing combining to form a picture of concentrated male authority.

A spurt of anger propelled her indoors. He had no right to look so—so unaffected! But once inside she stood for a long time staring blindly out to sea, wondering whether she was dealing with this whole situation wrongly. Her brows drew together. Was she wilfully throwing away her chance of finding a man she could learn to love?

Simone was not a coward, but her experience with Jason had made her more than cautious. Still, she had always hoped that one day she would find a man who would make her forget that period of her life, bewildering and frustrating as it had been, ending in tragedy. Perhaps she should see whether they were compatible in other ways besides the most basic.

Compared to Jason, Angus had a powerful, compelling personality, allied to a strength of will that made her a little fearful. There were other differences; Jason had never seen her as person. He had not fallen in love with Simone Atkinson, he had fallen in love with her body, and somehow he had managed to convince himself that only if he painted her over and over, obsessively setting that beautiful body, those features, on to canvas, without touching her, only then would his skill remain.

She had not known what to do. With no one to turn to, as Jason had insisted she give up modelling, she had struggled vainly against the dark whirlpool of his illness, striving to make sense of the contradictions he had treated as normal.

She shifted uneasily, remembering her fear, her bewilderment, the eventual hopelessness. He had sworn he loved her, had told her over and over how much he adored her, how vital she was to him, how he needed her more than life itself; but he had never talked to her, never made any attempt to find out how her mind worked. He'd treated her with a lofty arrogance, as though she had no intelligence, nothing to offer except her body and her face.

At last, exhausted, afraid, unable to think of any other way of getting through to him, she had threatened to leave, and his handsome face had tightened with contempt. 'So you're a slut just like the others,' he had sneered. 'You can't live without it, can you?'

Even now, all these years later, her memories of that final scene had the power to make her ache with shame and humiliation. He had called her names she had never heard before, and then he had dragged her off to bed.

But once there, he had been unable to do anything. He had blamed her for his impotence, erupting into a fury so extreme that she had been terrified. Slamming at last out of the apartment, he had snarled that he would find a woman on the street with more to offer than she had. Simone had taken the opportunity to flee all the way back to New Zealand.

Humiliated, traumatised, she had seen a lawyer and insisted on a legal separation. The documents had been found clutched in Jason's hand when he shot himself. The last portrait of her—nude, facing away from the onlooker with her long, elegant back exposed—had been what he'd looked at as he died.

It had been the most appalling scandal. She had appeared in the worst of the gutter Press; indeed, the stories they'd printed about her had been so outrageous that she had had to sue several of them. It was only when the courts awarded her large damages that the salacious, vicious rumours had come to an abrupt halt.

Simone swallowed, refusing to allow herself to feel the old, familiar horror. She had had to face the court; not even then had she admitted the empty horror of the marriage. She said that she left him because he refused to allow her to continue working.

Thank heavens they had accepted that. Perhaps because of the scandal she had been rushed off her feet with work, work she needed desperately to take her mind off the shambles she had made of her life. Eventually she had lived the whole sordid mess down, but it had left her with scars on her soul and a deep-seated fear of making any other commitment.

And Angus, she thought as she watched gulls diving out in the bay, Angus was not the sort of man to cut her teeth on. He excited her, but she was not experienced enough for him.

At the memory of that kiss exchanged in the sun she pressed a clenched hand to her breast, noting with dismay the sudden acceleration of her heartbeat. Experience or not, he had felt it too, that overwhelming hunger. Should she run back to her safe life, or should she stay, test the dangerous waters, see if she was strong enough to deal with them on their own terms?

She discovered that in some courageous inner part of her soul the decisions had already been made. It would be cowardly to run away.

During the afternoon she brought a lounger out on to the concrete terrace in front of the bach and lay back in it, letting the warmth soak into her bones while she read. Sinbad played with a fallen leaf at her feet. The kitten must have had some experience with humans, for, although she still spat and defended herself if Simone tried to pick her up, she didn't appear afraid of Simone's nearness. Especially as the saucer of milk was close by in a convenient patch of shade.

Simone chuckled at the little animal's antics, then slid so swiftly and smoothly into sleep that her wakening came as a great surprise. Angus was standing in front of her, Sinbad crouched beneath the lounger making those little spitting sounds.

'Oh, lord.' Replete with sun and sleep, Simone yawned, then yawned again. 'What's she done?'

'She was making a determined effort to get down to the beach. I managed to lure her back with a piece of dry grass, but I think it might be an idea to put her inside when you sleep.'

Colour tinged her skin as she struggled upright. 'I didn't even realise I was asleep,' she said drowsily, rubbing her heavy eyes.

His smile had more than a hint of irony. 'I know the feeling. Would you like to come for a walk along the beach?'

She sent him a long, considering look from beneath her lashes. The sensible thing to do would be to send him away, tell him that she didn't think it a good idea to see him again. 'Yes, I would,' she said with decision.

Five minutes later Sinbad was ensconced in the laundry eating a small amount of liver with every appearance of enjoyment, and Simone was rejoining the tall man who waited for her. He gave her a level, unsmiling look, ruffling the sensibilities she had tried so hard to settle, but said nothing beyond, 'A jacket might be a good idea. There's a cloud bank coming in from the north.'

She collected her padded jacket from her bedroom and rejoined him, suddenly far too aware of him and of her own quivering senses. Something had happened, something she wasn't going to be able to ignore. Physical attraction was one thing; this, she thought hollowly as she swung into step beside his tall, rangy figure, this was something else again.

Yet they had a pleasant walk. He asked her about the book she was reading, and when she began to discuss it he responded.

As they walked over the steep, sheep-cropped hills, the subject of their conversation ranged far and wide, from the agricultural surpluses bedevilling the world to politics and the arts, gardening and to his work.

Exhilarated, she didn't forget that this man had the power to make her world spin crazily on its axis; that would have been impossible, for somehow this meeting of minds enhanced that basic call of the flesh, gave it depth and texture, so that as her respect and admiration for his impressive mind grew she became more and more dizzily attracted.

And she didn't think quite so harshly of herself for that fiery response. Once she looked up, and saw his brilliant, burnished gaze on her mouth, and her eyes went smoky and seductive.

I want you, he had said, without speaking a syllable, and, I want you too, she had replied, in a language as old as time.

Fugitive colour tinged her cheeks, but he said nothing, and after a moment she went on talking. She was relieved at his circumspection; that restraint distinguished him from other men, who had often been insultingly blunt in their propositions, and insulted when she refused them. Jason had managed to talk her into marriage after only three weeks. Besotted and blinded by her first experience of passion, she had agreed eagerly to his pleading.

Well, she had learnt her lesson. Slow and steady, and before she admitted him into her heart she was going to make sure that she knew this man. Perhaps, she thought with a lilt in her heart, perhaps he was going to be the man who appealed to her on every level, instead of only one. Perhaps she could learn to love Angus Grey.

Perhaps he could learn to love the very fallible, ordinary person who was Simone Atkinson.

But it was too early to think of that; first they had to get to know each other.

He said in a neutral voice, 'I gather you like solitude.'

'Yes. You must, too.'

His shoulders lifted in the faintest of shrugs. 'Essentially, or so my sister tells me, I'm a loner.'

'So,' she said evenly, 'am I.'

He shook his head. Fascinated, she watched the sun deepen and intensify the colour of his hair, licking at it so that it glowed with an inner fire. 'Really?' he said drily. 'Your name appears frequently in the gossip columns.'

She shrugged, refusing to accept the subtle put-down. 'That's business. It pays to keep my name before the world. Anyway, I have work to do here, and I need the quietness.'

There, that should let him know that she didn't expect him to dance attendance on her.

He looked amused, obviously wondering just what work she intended to do at Wainui Cove. She could have told him of the small computer that stood in the spare bedroom, and the letter from the editor of an American publisher saying that the first three chapters and synopsis of her detective novel set in the world of high fashion were good, and that they wanted to see the rest of the book as soon as she could produce it. Over the last three months she had snatched the time to write the first two drafts and the next few weeks were going to be spent doing the final polishing.

But she wasn't going to tell him; she was a little shy of telling anyone. What if the editor didn't like the final manuscript? So far no one else knew what she was doing when she typed away in her room at night.

'Are you on holiday too?' she asked a little pertly.

'I suppose you could call it a holiday. I like the sea; it helps me to think. One of these days I'll buy a house on the coast.'

'I'd like that, too,' she said, wondering where she would settle when she came back this time next year. 'I love to wake at night and hear the waves on the beach. I wonder if humanity spent some of its earlier years beside some great sea, so that the sound of it is always in our hearts.'

'We all come from the sea,' he said. 'Our blood is almost the same composition as sea-water. We love it because for untold generations we lived in it.'

They had walked up a scrub-covered hill behind the bay and turned to look out over the magnificent panorama before them, of sea and islands, blue and green and silver beneath the sun. To the south the white marker of a trig-height gleamed above white rocks scattered over green grass on the tallest hill around, one cleared entirely of native vegetation to provide grass for sheep.

Between that hill and them was a valley, a deep gash in the hills with steep, bush-covered sides where soft white drifts of clematis veiled trees and the silver thread of a waterfall plummeted down a dark, rocky cleft. Secondary valleys snaked their way up into the hills, and on the floor of the valley were gardens, empty now of plants except for some rows of potatoes, but as soon as the soil warmed up sweet corn would be planted there, and kumara, the sweet potato that arrived in New Zealand with the Maori a thousand or so years ago. Along a steep, high ridge that fell to the valley on one side and the sea on the other the road climbed and snaked

before it disappeared between smooth, steep green paddocks high above the coast.

'This must be one of the best views in the world,'
Simone murmured, leaning back against the trunk of an
old pine tree and filling her eyes with their bounty of
beauty.

'Yes.' But Angus was looking at her.

She kept her eyes fixed on the shimmering melding of
sea and shore, and after a taut moment he too transferred his gaze out over their tiny cove to the glittering
promise of the sea.

From the corner of her eyes she caught movement,
and turned her head to the right, trying to see what
flashed among the trees. A frown tugged at her brows.

'What are you looking at?'

'I don't know. I just caught a flash—ah, yes, look,
there it is again.'

He caught her hand and pulled her close. Bewildered,
she stared up into his face. 'I saw it too,' he said. 'The
flash of the sun off a pair of binoculars.' He bent his
head and swiftly kissed her. 'Don't turn around, don't
struggle.'

She stood very still. 'You mean someone's watching
us?'

'Yes.' He kissed her again, hard, magical, making her
blood leap, then said in a cool, unemotional tone, 'Turn
away and point to the north, as though you're pointing
out something down on the farm to me.'

She obeyed him, uneasily conscious that they were
being watched, trying to rid herself of the uncomfortable sensations crawling across her skin.

'Who do you think it is?' she asked.

'Probably a perfectly innocent, though rude local
trying out his binoculars. However, there's no road there,
and this is the season for cannabis planting to begin.
Just in case, we'll pretend we haven't seen anything, and
the next time we go into Kerikeri I'll tell the police.'

'Ugh,' she said, suddenly cold.

He nodded. 'OK, let's go down the hill now. Don't not look there; be casual.'

'It's hard to be casual,' she muttered, unable to banish the ice that crept down her spine. But he seemed to manage it easily enough. In fact, she thought, looking up at him as he took her hand and smiled down at her, he seemed to be taking advantage of that suspicious flash of light to take all sorts of liberties.

Liberties she shouldn't grant him, because anticipation was sharpening her nerves to a hard edge, running from the loose, warm touch of his fingers up her arm and thence by a myriad pathways through every cell in her body.

'You look as though you're enjoying this,' she accused. 'And as though you're accustomed to it.'

He shrugged. 'I once got tangled up in an industrial espionage case, and had to do a bit of training with the police force. It was—interesting. And yes, it did satisfy a latent instinct for violence, I suppose. However, I was glad when it was over.'

'"A latent instinct for violence",' she mused, frowning. 'I don't like the sound of that.'

His smile was narrow and mirthless. 'Most men can be violent, given the right circumstances. Women, too.'

'Yes, I suppose so,' she sighed, thinking of one woman in particular—another model who had been dumped by the agency because she had tried to slap Simone senseless one day. 'But only in extreme circumstances, surely?'

'It's all right,' he told her gravely, 'I don't go around beating people up. In fact, I have good control over my baser instincts.'

Too good, perhaps. 'Don't you think perhaps you should go straight away to the police?'

'No. If by any chance they are planting cannabis they'll be there for some months yet.'

'I hate the thought of anyone watching me.'

'Yet that's how you earn your living.'

'That's different,' she murmured. 'Why do you dislike models so? And don't try to tell me that you don't; I sensed it when I saw you on the street at Virginia City. Your dislike scorched the air.'

'I think you're being a little melodramatic!' But the deep, hard note in his voice was a little raw, as though she had surprised him.

'Give me credit for some instincts,' she said drily.

He shrugged. 'My ex-wife was a model.'

It was then that Simone realised she was in real trouble. She had never been jealous before, never experienced a single pang of that distasteful emotion, but it seared through her now, primitive, ferocious, so painful that she had to stop herself from gasping with it.

'I gather it was not an amicable divorce,' she said when she could summon the fortitude to speak.

'No.'

'And so all models are tarred with the same brush?'

'No.' He picked up her hand and kissed it, his tongue moving delicately across her lifeline in a caress that sent delicious little shudders rippling through her. 'Or at least I hope not. But that day in Virginia City you reminded me a little of her, and I was taken by surprise.'

Her fingers curled, cupping his mouth. It took a real effort to loosen them, to give her hand the little tug necessary to drag it back from that seductive caress. 'Do I look like her?'

He shrugged, the mask of control set firmly over his features. 'Not really. She had red hair, about the same length as yours, and green eyes, as well as that exquisite skin. She was tall, too, but you are a couple of inches or so taller. I reacted badly, but it was mainly shock.'

She reacted to the dismissive note in his voice with something like pain, and cursed herself for it. Her hand was still lying resistlessly in his; she let it stay while she murmured, 'I don't like collecting emotions for another woman. It makes me feel as though I'm nothing but an assortment of physical features.'

'And yet you set yourself up for that kind of opinion.'

She withdrew her hand firmly. 'Perhaps, to those people who don't understand what sheer hard work modelling can be, and how much acting ability is necessary to get you through. It is not merely standing around with half an inch of make-up on your face looking glamorous——'

'All right,' he said, smiling a little at her vehemence. 'You're forgetting that I saw a little of your work, and I'll agree that it's certainly not passive, or so simple that anyone can do it. But you must admit that you wouldn't be there without your stunning physical attributes.'

'There are plenty of women who look better than I do, who have bodies that are every bit as good as mine for photographing,' she returned smartly. 'A lot of them start off as models, but not many get to the top. It needs hard work and reliability and common sense, as well as the physical attributes. And really, the only physical attribute you need is the fashionable body shape of the period; you certainly don't need to be beautiful. But you do need to have that certain something that the camera likes.'

'And luck?' he suggested in a neutral voice that made her look sharply up into his uncommunicative face, wondering exactly what he meant.

'And luck,' she agreed woodenly. 'That applies to life, doesn't it?'

He shrugged. 'I suppose so.'

'But you don't think so.' She smiled rather ironically. 'OK, what was it, other than luck, that saw you born healthy and strong in a country like New Zealand, where you were positively encouraged to make the most of yourself?'

He acknowledged blandly, 'I'll grant you that amount of luck. After that, I think we make our lives to a much greater extent than most believe. I've heard people bemoaning their luck, wasting away their lives because they believe they're unlucky, when anyone with an ounce of sense could see that they're making their own bad luck by being lazy, or thoughtless, or careless.'

'I agree, but that's a fairly tough sort of philosophy if you apply it to everyone without exception. What about people who crash in a plane?'

His broad shoulders moved in a shrug. 'I'm not talking about that sort of cosmic accident, as you're well aware!'

Laughing, she tossed her head, unaware of the way the sun gleamed and glittered on her fall of hair, turning it into liquid fire about her tantalising face. 'I was teasing,' she said. 'And I'm inclined to believe you, although I think that luck has a place in any life. To say that we lead the life we deserve is a crushing, almost inhumane belief.'

Angus's eyes had sharpened but his voice was casual as he returned, 'Inhumane? Why, because it takes away the soft cushion of helplessness against the vagaries of cruel fate, and puts the onus fair and square where it belongs, on each individual?'

'Some people have undeserved bad and good luck,' she argued, thinking of her mother. 'And what about coincidence, for example? What about the fact that, after spending our lives up until now very happily not having met, we run across each other twice in less than a month, half a world apart? How does that fit into your philosophy?'

'It was bound to happen,' he said, returning her challenging look with a cynical smile. 'New Zealand is notorious for coincidences, you know that. Except that what most people see as coincidences are really perfectly logical happenings because the country is so small and so isolated. We're continually tripping over each other. As for meeting you in Virginia City, I was told in Reno that there was a New Zealand outfit shooting up there, so I came up to see if I knew anyone.'

She sent him a laughing green glare. 'I refuse to admit that life is as mundane as that,' she said firmly, noting with fascination how the sun picked out the cleft in his chin. 'You think your way and I'll think mine.'

'So you don't feel that you've made your own luck?'

'Not entirely. I was exceedingly fortunate that my mother sent in the photograph of me to the modelling contest, fortunate that I'm one of those people whom the camera loves. And that my sort of face and body have been fashionable these last ten years.'

'So what are you going to do when the world gets over its love affair with Simone? Or when gravity and time start the slow ruin of that exquisite, inviting beauty, as they must sooner or later?'

She wasn't ready to tell him. 'Oh, I'll find something to do,' she said vaguely.

'Here, or overseas?'

She chuckled. 'All New Zealanders come back home, you know that.' She gestured at the glowing, opalescent expanse of sea before them, the golden beach and the rocks, the line of small islands that sheltered the bay. 'This,' she said softly, 'is worth all the cities in the world.'

'For a holiday, yes,' he said cynically.

She frowned, but didn't correct him. Would she be happy to live in such isolation, beautiful though it was? She admitted that she didn't know. She loved so much of the cities she had just so sweepingly condemned—the art, theatre and music, and yes, the gossip and excitement.

Yet she had never been so thrilled by a painting as she was by nature, and, for all that she enjoyed company and friends, she always felt that some inner part of her, some hidden core, stood aloof.

Perhaps that was why she enjoyed Angus's company. Because he too was reserved, some part of him shielded from too easy understanding.

In some ways they were alike.

And in others, she thought, her eyes drifting down the lean male magnificence of his body, he was splendidly different. A silent, rushing tide of sensation flowed through her, dizzying her with happiness. No, it was more than happiness; the day, and the man, the scenery and the fresh, salty air combined to produce an elation unlike anything she had ever experienced before.

CHAPTER FIVE

BACK at the cove Angus said with a casualness that didn't quite hide the fact that he meant every word, 'If you hear or see anything that worries you, let me know, won't you? You can ring from your unit to mine quite easily.'

And that sneaking tide of unease was back, banishing Simone's iridescent delight. 'Do you think——?'

'No,' he interrupted decisively. 'I don't. I'm certain we have no need to worry at all. Even if they were up to no good there, the last thing they'd want to do is call attention to themselves in any way. That said, promise me that if anything alarms you you'll let me know.'

She hesitated, and he said coaxingly, 'Please, Simone.'

It was difficult to relinquish control of her life in even that small instance, but she recognised the look in his eyes. If she didn't agree, he'd keep a watch on her. He was, she thought with debilitating pleasure, an instinctively protective man. In its way that was just as dangerous as the aura of male potency she had been resisting since she had first seen him.

'Yes, all right,' she said simply.

He smiled, and although something was still held in reserve she almost swooned at his feet. Like that, the dark charisma lightened by amusement and understanding, he was desperately attractive.

'Good girl,' he said, chuckling when she automatically stiffened. 'Yes, I know, but admit it, good woman doesn't have that smooth flow, and sounds even more patronising! And just in case——' He bent, and kissed her, lightly yet with a hint of the hidden intensity that fascinated her. Lips lingering on hers, he murmured, 'Perhaps we had better continue to look like very good friends.'

Simone's body responded with such blazing ardour that she had difficulty formulating any sort of reply to this open enticement. Instead she stepped back, gave him a long, measuring look which he met with bland arrogance, and said gruffly, 'No one can see us now unless they're out at sea,' before disappearing into the unit to the sound of his soft laughter.

She stood for a long moment pressing the backs of her fingers to her hot cheeks. Curled in a pool of sunlight on the divan, Sinbad woke and yawned, stretching, her small claws reflexively kneading into the material of the cover.

'No, don't do that,' Simone scolded, picking up the soft little bundle. For the first time the kitten didn't object. Instead, she stayed loose and relaxed, and swiped Simone's hand with a surprisingly rough little tongue.

It was soothing to sit down with the kitten in her lap and stroke the soft, warm fur, trace the delicate ears, the lines of deeper and paler colouring along the gently rising ribs. Sinbad went back to sleep again, little white paws folded delicately beneath her, the disparate eyes closing.

'What on earth is happening to me?' Simone whispered, and couldn't stop herself from sending a furtive look over her shoulder just in case Angus was still outside the unit.

Of course he wasn't; the beach was empty.

Emboldened, Simone confided to the sleeping kitten, 'I've never felt like this before. But I don't know what he feels for me. Oh, there's an attraction; he tries to hide it, but it's there, I can sense it. Only—is it me, or is it the fact that I look like his ex-wife? Clearly he's attracted to our physical type. Which is about the most unflattering thing that's ever happened to me!'

Sinbad opened her eyes and yawned, then settled down again. Simone went on, still in the same soft voice, 'But although he makes my toes curl, Sinbad, it can't possibly be love, not in such a short time. I'm not going to make another mistake. We have three weeks to get to know each other. By then I should have discovered whether he just sees me as an available woman, or whether his feelings are deeper than that.'

She stroked down the delicate backbone, feeling the warmth, the tiny throbbing life beneath the sensitive pad of her finger. 'I hope they are,' she whispered, alarmed because until that moment she hadn't realised just how much she hoped.

If only it weren't so difficult to tell what he was thinking! They were like shadow actors, playing behind a screen, so lifelike that they fooled most people, but with the essential clues concealed so that their deepest emotions, the ones that prowled in the darker regions of their hearts, were caged and hidden.

Simone knew why she was like that, but what had made Angus so careful? The ex-wife? She tried to remember the tone of his voice when he'd spoken of her, but as usual he had given nothing away. The divorce had not been amicable, and it was clear that he had few pleasant memories of the woman he had married; but why? Why had she left him?

What had Paula Bishop said about the woman? Not much—only that she had the same colouring as Simone, but not what it took to be a real success. In other words, Simone decided with a wry smile, she lacked stamina, or a level head, or discretion. If she really had married Angus for his money, it was probably all three.

As the sun went down the western sky she sat stroking the little kitten, wondering just why the marriage had failed. If Angus hated his ex-wife so much that he was prepared to dislike on sight a woman who looked vaguely like her and shared the same occupation, it didn't augur well for any shared future.

If his attraction was reluctant, merely a quirk of sexual desire, then Simone admitted she was hoping for the moon. He would probably enjoy an affair with her, but that would be all. And an affair was not what she wanted.

She would rather leave now than go through the pain of learning to love him, and have to watch him walk away from her.

But he enjoyed her company, she was sure of it. She kept her end up; she had managed to shock him a couple of times, she had forced him to admit that she was an intelligent human being. Had his wife perhaps been a lovely dim-wit, relying solely on her looks?

If that was so, Simone could understand his reaction; he was a proud man, and he would despise himself for falling in love with nothing more than a woman's face and body.

Well, he would soon learn that her outward appearance, pleasant though it was, was not all that Simone had to offer.

'Not even the most part,' she told Sinbad firmly, deciding that she wasn't going to be a coward. She might never meet another man who had the power to turn her bones to honey, so she was going to see this through. Angus Grey would learn that there was far more to her than her looks and sleek, fashionable body type!

With a smile that was a mixture of determination and surprise at her own temerity, she finally put Sinbad back on to the divan and went about making dinner. Tomorrow, she promised herself, she would start on the editing of her manuscript.

Sinbad slept on the bed with her again that night, and spent the next golden morning playing with a piece of newspaper tied to a length of string, batting it with her white paws, crouching and springing, killing it with instinctive facility. Simone was fascinated, but after a few minutes forced herself to work, determinedly shutting out the kitten's antics, and the far more disturbing knowledge that Angus Grey was only a few metres away in the next bach.

With a discipline that had been painfully acquired she worked until midday, when she made herself a chicken and avocado and lettuce sandwich and a cup of tea, and took them out on to the little terrace with its lounger and umbrella. Sinbad found a leaf and spent an eminently satisfactory time stalking it, while Simone admitted gloomily that the hero of her book was beginning to assume a few character traits that seemed suspiciously like the man next door's.

She would have to fight against that. Lettuce crunched satisfactorily between her teeth as she demolished her sandwich, staring with unseeing eyes at the glittering water.

A dinghy came into view around the rocks at the end of the cove. Idly she watched it, until she realised two things. One was that the man whose casual strength sent the oars so smoothly through the water was Angus, and the other—that he was wearing nothing more than a pair of shorts, their faded blue indicating a start in life as jeans.

Simone was wearing sunglasses, but even so embarrassment brought a wash of colour to her skin. As though he could tell that she was watching with helpless fascination, avid eyes lingering on the sleek muscles as they flexed and coiled beneath the smooth bronze skin! Her mouth dried. He must, she thought, spend a lot of time out in the sun to get that colour.

Once in shallow water he leapt over the side and began to drag the dinghy up on to the sand. Simone put down her sandwich and raced down to help him.

'It's all right,' he said as she came up, his eyes flicking dismissively over long legs clad in jungle-green trousers. 'You'll get yourself wet.'

She lifted an ironic brow and went around to the stern, but although she pushed with all her weight she still couldn't keep her eyes away from his sheer masculine power, arrogant in its complete unaffectedness. She suspected he took his magnificent body totally for granted.

For the first time she appreciated how her own good looks must affect the men who wanted her. She could even sympathise a little, for it was not the effort she was expending that shortened her breath and set her heart beating double time.

'OK, it's above the high-water mark,' he said. He waited until she had straightened up before continuing calmly, 'Thank you. Would you like a fish for dinner?'

Her gaze fell on the two fish in the bottom of the boat. 'Snapper!' she said, smiling. 'I'd love one, thank you.'

'I'll scale it and fillet it and bring it over.'

She chuckled, suddenly very happy. 'I can scale and fillet it for myself,' she said demurely, her smile widening as she saw the quickly hidden surprise in his expression. 'My father was a fisherman. He taught me how to deal with any fish he caught. But why don't you bring them both over and I'll make dinner for us?'

She sensed his withdrawal even before he said, perfectly pleasantly but with a definite note of refusal that chilled her, 'That's very kind of you, but not tonight, I'm afraid.'

Nodding, she refused to let him see how much his rebuff hurt. Had she become spoilt and conceited? Perhaps she deserved to be turned down occasionally.

Did he think that the kisses he had given her yesterday might have made her possessive, clinging?

But she had learnt something. Angus Grey liked to be the one who hunted, not the one who was chased. Had his ex-wife chased him? And then rejected him in the most wounding way known to a man?

Beneath the tangle of her racing thoughts Simone worried, because his rebuff had hurt her more than anything she had experienced for a long time. I must not become too dependent on him, she decided, frowning, because there didn't seem to be any way to stop it, short of running away. And that was cowardly.

The snapper was delicious; both she and Sinbad enjoyed it, although Simone had to consciously force herself to. Angus had not gone out; the Range Rover remained in the car-port.

She was not going to presume again.

She would work, and lie in the sun, and rest, and be perfectly pleasant, and if he wanted to further their acquaintance he could make any effort that was needed. She wasn't going to.

Anyway, she had an excellent excuse for not seeing him until the memory of that definite snub had lost a little of its pain; tomorrow afternoon Sinbad was booked into the clinic at Kerikeri for her innoculations and a check-up.

That night, as she lay in bed with the kitten asleep under the duvet at the end of the bed, she wept for her mother, and, she realised with a shock, for Jason. It was the first time she had been able to grieve for him; when he died she had been so exhausted, so bewildered and shocked, that she had only been able to think of him as he affected her emotions. Now, for the first time, she saw his life for the tragedy it had been—one character flaw, pride, dragging down a man who could have been one of the world's great artists.

After his death she had gone to his doctor, driven by her need to know whether he had been impotent, or whether he had been right, and she was unable to attract a man. The doctor, a sleek, composed man, had looked at her for a long time, clearly weighing up whether he was entitled to break the rule of patient confidentiality. He had listened to her halting, scarlet-faced description of their marriage, and he had sighed.

'He came to me a year ago,' he said at last. 'He had been impotent then for several months. I could find no physical reason for it but he refused to do anything about it. From what I could gather, I assume that he was worried that analysis might take away his ability to paint. When you married him, I assumed that the problem had been overcome.'

She had been so angry with Jason, so insecure and shamed, that she had hated him for his arrogance, but now she thought she understood him a little better.

If he had admitted his impotence and sought help for it, instead of refusing to accept that he needed help, he could have learned how to deal with it. But his self-image had depended on the necessity for him to be flawless, and so he had been unable to do anything but punish himself in the most final way possible—death.

Her part in it had been incidental, Simone thought wryly. He had not loved her, he had loved to paint her; it could have been any woman.

Ironic, to think that he had wanted her only for the body he had painted with such passionate desperation, while Angus Grey was deeply suspicious of her because she bore more than a passing resemblance to his ex-wife. If she had been conceited about her looks that would certainly show her how little she had to be proud of!

She worked hard the next morning, and half of the afternoon. By lunchtime rain was falling, not heavily, but with persistence. It was still falling at three when she lured Sinbad into the cat basket and stood, car keys in her hand, hesitating. Her tongue touched her top lip; with a shake of her head she went across to the telephone.

Angus answered, his voice hard and remote.

'Do you want anything in Kerikeri?' she asked, pleasantly but distantly. 'I'm taking Sinbad in to the vet, so if there's anything you need I could get it while I'm there.'

At the end of a moment's silence he said, 'No, thank you.'

'OK.' She hung up and stood for a moment surveying the phone. Then her wide shoulders lifted in a shrug and she swung the car keys as she went out through the door. He couldn't have made it more plain that he was regretting those kisses, that closeness.

Well, he didn't have to freeze her off to show her that she shouldn't get her hopes up! She wasn't going to intrude any more on Angus Grey's life!

To the kitten's great indignation Sinbad was vaccinated, then checked over before being pronounced fit and well, although a trifle too thin. Simone packed her back into the cat basket and bought flea powder and vitamin and bone meal supplements. In the intensifying rain she drove down to the supermarket and chose groceries and meat, enough for her and the cat, found some magazines in a bookshop, then filled the car up with petrol before driving carefully back along the road that took her to Wainui Cove.

It needed all her concentration, for once she was off the sealed road the rain had made the road slippery, in some places almost dangerous.

She was driving slowly and extremely carefully along the narrow ridge before the bay when a car came sliding around the corner on her side, so completely out of control that the driver had his hands off the wheel. The last thing she saw before the impact was the faces of the two men in the front, horrified, their eyes huge.

There was a grating crunch, a wild spinning of the cosmos around her, and then, a long time later, silence.

Simone drew in a deep, ragged breath. The cars had collided, and hers had tipped right over on one side, imprisoning her. The seatbelt that held her suspended seemed to have saved her from injury; just to make sure, she frantically moved all the relevant bits of her anatomy, sighing with relief when each one worked without pain. Hastily she switched off the key. From the back she could hear Sinbad mewing with an indignation that seemed to indicate she hadn't been hurt.

Thank heavens she had cinched one of the seatbelts in the back around the little basket! Sinbad's cries faded into silence. Simone tried to turn around, but could see nothing.

There were noises from outside, several men's voices, quick and alarmed, just out of hearing so that she couldn't make out what they were saying.

'Hey!' she shouted. But the only sound she heard was the receding engine as the vehicle that had hit her fled along the ridge towards the main road.

She dragged in her breath in a deep, sobbing gasp, terrified at being left like this. A sharp pain in her neck made her wince and turn her head slowly. A further gentle exploration revealed a bump on her temple; she must have hit her head when the car tipped over.

The rain poured in through the shattered windscreen; she opened her eyes, narrowing them to peer through the thickening light, and saw, with a chill that brought her out in a cold sweat, that over the bonnet she could see nothing. At least half the car was suspended out beyond the edge of the road.

Her teeth clamped hard on to her bottom lip, drawing blood. She didn't dare move. How much of the car was over the bank? What would it take to tip the whole thing over, so that she and the kitten plunged three or four hundred feet in a juddering, scrambling rush through the scrub down into the valley below?

She had never felt so alone, so afraid. The rain eased a little, and through the shattered window came the sweet honey fragrance of the shrubs on the side of the road, intense, almost musky on the wet air.

What if someone came around the corner from behind and drove right into her? The sudden thought made her tense into rigidity. She forced herself to relax. With a wet road and the rain still pouring down no local would be going so fast that they couldn't stop. And it was getting too late in the day for tourists. But why had the men in the other car driven off so cruelly?

Her mind rushed back to the flash of the binoculars. Surely they hadn't lain in wait—no, of course they hadn't. Fighting back tears of loneliness and shock and fear, she ordered herself to be calm, to think. Someone would be along soon.

'Sinbad?' she said softly.

There was a faint scratching noise from the back, but no answer. 'Perhaps you should have been a dog,' she whispered on a sob, 'then at least you could have whined. I'm afraid they're going to have to cut us out. But at

least we're up here, not down in the tea-tree at the bottom
of the hill, all smashed up!'

Sudden tears blinded her; she sniffed and swallowed,
calling on all her self-command to compose herself.
Carrying on like a hysteric would be totally counter-
productive. Eyes darting around the car, she strove desperately to find some way of getting herself and the kitten
out.

Unfortunately, there didn't seem to be one. If she
moved too much she could well send them both to their
death down the hillside.

With a cold, desperate courage she settled to wait it
out. The rain thrummed in through the shattered windscreen, wetting her so that she soon began to shiver. She
breathed slowly and deeply as the afternoon wore its way
slowly towards evening.

It seemed hours before she heard the faint sound of
an engine, and even then she didn't dare hope. She had
heard that same sound at least three times, and each
time nothing had come of it. She was profoundly uncomfortable, held in place with the tough material of
the seatbelt cutting ever further into the soft skin of her
shoulder and hip. But she managed to whisper her fervent
thanks when at last she was sure the vehicle was on its
way up the hill towards her.

She braced herself as it came around the corner, its
lights like solid beams cutting through the rain, only re-
laxing when it came to a halt with a skid that dried her
throat. A door slammed; she heard the crunch of gravel
as feet raced across the road.

And then she recognised Angus's deep voice, and the
relief was like sweet wine running through her veins.

'Simone,' he said harshly. 'Oh, lord, Simone!'

'Oh, Angus, thank God...' Her voice was weak. She
swallowed, and said more firmly, 'I'm all right.'

'I'll get a rope on to you,' he told her swiftly, his voice
once more under control, although the deep, raw note

that gave it its curiously sexual flavour had hardened into a crisp authority that eased her fear immediately.

'Good idea,' she croaked.

He worked swiftly, telling her what he was doing so that she didn't feel so cut off, and within a few minutes he was back, saying, 'There, you're tied to the Range Rover and to a decent-sized totara tree through the fence on the other side of the road. I've put out accident cones, so you're perfectly safe now. Are you hurt?'

'No,' she said, ironing out the wobble in the words before it had a chance to betray her. 'I don't think I'm at all hurt, though I'm sick and tired of hanging like this.'

There was an odd pause, before he said in a voice she wouldn't have recognised, 'Wriggle your toes.'

She gulped and smiled through her foolish tears. 'I've done all that; I've wriggled all my toes and my arms and fingers, and they all work without any pain. Just a few aches and bruises. I can breathe without any difficulty.'

'OK.' His voice was calm and confident, reassuring her that all was well. Some last piece of her sensible mind scoffed at this, but she gave in, leaning gratefully on his in-built authority.

'Now listen,' he said, 'I'm going to go back to the bay to get help——'

He stopped, as the sound of another engine, this time from the other direction, burgeoned through the rain. 'Hang on there,' he said.

Almost immediately she heard the motor stop, followed by the thud of a door slamming shut to the accompaniment of a pleasant male voice. Then Angus's voice, succinct, very much to the point. Within a very short time it became obvious that the newcomer, whoever he was, was automatically awarding leadership to Angus. A stupid sob thickened her throat, but she gritted her teeth and waited.

'Simone,' Angus said calmly, once more back beside the car, 'Jim is going to ring for help on his carphone.

Hang on for a while longer, we'll have you out of there as soon as we can.'

He stayed talking to her through all the fuss that followed—the arrival of the fire engine with its equipment for cutting her out, the interview with both the police and the traffic officer when she was finally free, even the quick check-over by a doctor who pronounced her shocked, but in good shape.

'We can send you off to the hospital for the night,' the doctor suggested.

'She'll be all right at home,' Angus interposed smoothly, draping a rug around her shoulders. His hands stayed on her shoulders, supporting her. 'Unless you'd feel better if you went in?'

She shook her head, leaning back a little so that she could rest against the hard wall of his chest. Now that it was all over she had to fight off a series of shudders.

The doctor gave him an envious look and said a little too heartily, 'OK, then, no need to worry. Just keep warm and go straight to bed.'

By then the ruined car had been hitched on to a tow-truck and dragged away, leaving nothing but the glittering heap of glass from the windscreen and a pool of oil on the road. Angus said, 'Hop into the Rover,' as he went with the doctor to his car, but Simone stayed where she was, looking at the pool of oil, so close to the edge.

She could no longer keep the shuddering at bay. Sinbad, who had been extracted with the groceries and magazines, like them completely unharmed, yowled a couple of times from the Range Rover, then fell silent.

With something like a leap in her heart she saw Angus's tall figure silhouetted against the lights of the other vehicles, and succumbed to a clutch of relief.

'You should be in the Rover,' he said as he came towards her.

She sniffed and nodded. 'Yes. I know. I was—I was just looking at the oil.'

He knew immediately what she meant, and pulled her close, holding her against his broad chest in the classical position for comfort. For a moment she let her forehead rest against the taut line of his jaw, assailed by a wish that she could just let down her defences and give in. But she couldn't, and she drew back, looking half shyly upwards.

In the half-darkness it was difficult to catch his exact expression, but for a moment a headlight lit up his face, and revealed a bleak severity, the white line around the sculpted lips.

'Come on,' he said, 'I'll take you home.'

He took off his heavy woollen jacket and, after removing the blanket from around her shoulders, draped it, still warm from his body, faintly scented with the ineradicable male fragrance that was his alone, around her.

The policeman came up to her. 'There are just a few things——' he began pleasantly.

Just as pleasantly, but with an inflexible note that made Simone look sharply at him, Angus interrupted, 'She's almost out on her feet. If you want to ask her any more questions, how about leaving it until tomorrow?'

The policeman grinned. 'No problems there,' he said. 'I'll give you a ring tomorrow, Miss Atkinson.'

'Thank you,' she replied, smiling at him.

Angus picked her up and sat her in the front seat of the Range Rover. He said something to the policeman that made them both laugh, and then swung lithely around the front of the car. Simone sighed and relaxed.

He carried her into her unit, too, sat her on one of the divans, and said calmly, 'Don't move. I'll get the fire going and then you can have a shower. I'll make up a bed in the spare room and spend tonight here, just to reassure myself that you're all right.'

'You seem to spend your time rescuing me from stupid situations. Believe me, I'm not normally so accident prone, or so——'

A lean finger stroked across her faintly mutinous mouth, stopping the words at the back of her throat. 'Just do as you're told,' he commanded, smiling, his dark eyes compelling.

Tiny shivers of what had to be exhaustion shuddered through her. She fought back the urge to kiss his finger and said obediently, 'All right.'

He said authoritatively, 'I'll make you a hot drink and something to eat. Don't be long in the bathroom.'

It was blissful to wash off the fear in the spray of water, although she grimaced a little at the bruises already beginning to show on her shoulder and hip. However, the seatbelt had done what it was supposed to. She didn't even want to think of what might have happened if she hadn't been wearing it.

Moving slowly, for aches and pains were catching up with her now, she washed her hair, then got carefully out of the bath and dried herself down.

'I wonder if they supply liniment here,' she said out loud.

A moment later Angus said from outside the door, 'What did you want?'

She clutched the towel around her. 'Nothing,' she called.

He stayed for a moment, then said, 'OK,' and presumably moved away, although she didn't hear anything.

Slowly, she went back to drying herself, suddenly far too hot. She towel-dried her hair and brushed it, catching it back in a pony-tail to keep it off her face. The dressing-gown tied high at her throat, its iridescent green almost the same colour as her eyes. She was pale, but apart from the bruising at her shoulder and hip no one would have realised that she had just spent the last hours pinned in her car on the edge of a cliff.

'Simone, hurry up in there.'

Smiling, she obeyed the imperative command, and walked out, oddly shy.

'You look about fifteen,' he commented drily, sitting her in the big armchair before he handed her a mug.

In a husky voice she said, 'I haven't thanked you——'

'You don't need to thank me.'

She continued blankly, only just realising that he had been on his way out when he'd found her, 'Weren't you going somewhere when you found me? Shouldn't you ring someone?'

'I came looking for you,' he said curtly. And when she stared at him he shrugged. 'You were late. You should have been home. I thought you might have broken down.'

A drenching sweetness burst inside her. After yesterday's rebuff his consideration was like manna to the Israelites.

'That was kind of you,' she said.

'It was merely neighbourly.'

She summoned a wry smile. 'I know perfectly well that you'd have done the same for anyone, but I—well, I was getting rather desperate there for a while.'

He lifted his brows, surveying her face keenly. 'You had every right to feel a little desperate. I did myself when I realised how close you were to going over the edge.'

'You didn't show it,' she said, wondering whether he really meant it.

'Neither did you.'

'It wouldn't have helped, would it?'

'No,' he said quietly, 'I don't suppose it would have. But you showed great courage and presence of mind, nevertheless.'

Colour tinged her high cheekbones. 'I had help,' she reminded him.

'Drink up your tea. I've got soup heating, and I'll make you an omelette after that. Then I think you'd better get off to bed. I'll put your electric blanket on.'

To her surprise and more than a little dismay Simone found that she liked being taken care of. It could, she thought sadly, even become addictive, the way Angus did it.

She thought she would stay awake for hours reliving that moment when she'd seen the edge of the road teeter before her horrified eyes, but he had soothed her fears so well that she dropped straight off to sleep.

However, she paid for this later in the night, when she woke with a heart pounding and the sound of her own scream in her ears as she struggled to break free of the nightmare.

'Hush,' Angus said deeply, pulling her into his arms as she lay rigid and sweat-soaked. 'It's all right, Simone, it's just a dream.'

She clutched him, turning her face into his throat, trying to bury herself in the rock-steady masculine competence she knew she could rely on. His arms tightened about her, holding the terrors at bay; she relaxed as his cheek came down on the top of her head. After long moments her breathing eased and her heart began to beat in time with his, slow and steady, as fundamental a rhythm as the pulse of the universe. He was wearing nothing but a pair of briefs; she could feel the heat and smell the faint salt tang of his body.

'I'm sorry,' she said in a muffled voice.

'Why? You're entitled to a nightmare or two.' He eased her back into the bed.

More than anything she wanted him to stay, but of course she couldn't say so. 'Thank you,' she said, hating the involuntary wobble in her voice.

He sat very still on the edge of the bed, then, as if making up his mind, pulled the blankets back and got in with her.

'Turn over,' he said briskly.

When she was lying with her back to him he curled around her spoon fashion and said quietly, 'Now, go back to sleep.'

And to her astonishment she did just that, sleeping soundly for the rest of the night, both body and mind accepting that she was completely safe.

She was alone when she woke, but from somewhere she could hear Angus's voice, and almost immediately he came into the bedroom, accompanied by Sinbad, clearly none the worse for her adventure.

'How are you feeling this morning?' he asked, apparently not at all embarrassed by the fact that they had spent the night together.

Simone kept her eyes on the kitten as she climbed up on to the bed. 'I'm fine,' she said carefully, aware that her hair was a tangled mess around her shoulders, and that her face no doubt showed the aftermath of yesterday's accident and the subsequent nightmare.

He approached the bed as silently as the kitten. With enormous eyes she watched as his finger beneath her chin lifted her face so that he could look straight into it. She saw beneath the harsh mask he wore now, saw to the essential goodness and compassion in him, the emotions he kept so firmly hidden, and her lashes drooped.

'Yes,' he said, amusement creasing his cheeks, 'you look yourself again.' Gently but inexorably he turned back the collar of her nightgown so that he could see the bruising in her soft flesh. His eyes darkened into obsidian. Very carefully he touched the slightly swollen skin. Then he released her, saying casually, 'That looks nasty, but it's not going to leave any permanent scar.' He folded the collar back and smiled into her startled eyes. 'Do you want breakfast in bed?'

'No, thank you. I'll be out in ten minutes.'

The accident marked a change in him, at first so minuscule that for a while she thought it just the gentleness of a very strong man for someone temporarily weaker than himself.

He began to spend most of each day with her, talking to her, making her laugh, teasing her, and even when she was obviously better he didn't leave her to her own devices as she had feared he would.

A kind of radiant hope began to break through the layers of suspicion she had cloaked herself with ever since her doomed marriage. Slowly it was borne in on her that he seemed to be showing a fundamental change of attitude. He relaxed with her, displaying a dry, ironic wit that often had her laughing helplessly.

Simone was fascinated by him—by his strength, his gentleness, the leashed sensuality he kept so firmly under control. She thought she could never tire of looking at the compelling lines and angles of his face, of hearing his deep voice with its intriguing hint of passion, watching from half-closed eyes his spare masculine grace. She didn't even wonder whether she was falling in love; for the first time in her life she was content to drift through the warm days of spring with a lazy, feline appreciation that kept a small, satisfied smile perpetually warming the cool green of her gaze.

Life had never seemed so good. They went fishing, and she showed him how good she was with a sharp knife, scaling and filleting like the expert she was. He rowed her around the bay, showing her small coves where the water ran up through black rocks and across the amber sand to huge old pohutukawa trees with their rough branches swooping down to kiss the water.

He enjoyed picnics, so almost every day they had a picnic somewhere, and she loved watching his strong white teeth demolish the food, while he teased her about her appetite, sharpened by the warm air and the exercise. Sinbad often came with them, apparently not in the least interested in going back to the wild.

'Cats know which side their bread is buttered on,' Angus said, and his eyes were cool and introspective as he watched the kitten play with a piece of seaweed.

'She likes me,' Simone retorted indignantly.

He looked up, his expression almost pitying. 'Not much,' he said. 'It's their nature; they're solitary beasts in the wild. They rely on no one, trust no one.'

Simone didn't want to believe it, but she had to admit that it could be true. Not without a hint of sympathy, he smiled, and changed the subject.

She didn't get much work done on her manuscript, but somehow the urgency was gone; each blue and gold day beckoned her outside to play, and the tall dark man who was gradually learning to be not so sparing of his smiles was taking over more and more of her time.

They became good friends, with that maverick attraction firmly controlled. Sometimes Simone chafed at his fundamental aloofness, while accepting it as part of his nature. Yet she delighted in his friendship, for she sensed that few people ever gained it. And always that deep, unexpressed awareness ran like a submerged, dangerous current between them. Yet they did not touch each other, taking great care to avoid it. It seemed, she thought, even as she admitted that she would like to take the next perilous step, that he too wanted to take things slowly, quietly.

Surely it indicated that this meant more to him than the usual relationship?

She knew that some day there would come a reckoning, but for now she was content to wander with him through the sweet, lazy days, learning a little of the way he thought, the way he reacted.

And then he said one day, 'I'm going to Auckland tomorrow. Will you be all right by yourself?'

It was like being slapped in the face. But she answered cheerfully, 'Yes, of course I will.'

He nodded, that shrewd gaze fixed on her averted face. 'Good. I'll be away for four or five days.'

He left before she was up the next morning, and that day she learned just how much he had become entwined with the fabric of her life. Loneliness ached as deep as her bones, but that night Mr Jackson, the farmer who

owned the baches, came down on his tractor; he saw her
walking along the beach and stopped to chat. She
thought nothing of it, until his wife called in the next
day, ostensibly to give her a bunch of brilliant ultra-
marine irises.

Simone said, 'Oh, they are beautiful! Thank you so
much.'

Mrs Jackson smiled. 'Yes, they are, aren't they? How
are things going?'

Simone looked up sharply. An incredible suspicion
formed full-blown in her brain. 'Mrs Jackson, did Angus
ask you to keep an eye on me?'

The older woman chuckled. 'Yes, but we would have,
anyway.'

It was clear what she thought. Fighting back a ridicu-
lous blush, Simone said sternly, 'It's very kind of you,
but really, I've been looking after myself for some years.'

'And very well, I've no doubt.' Mrs Jackson was
soothing, but nevertheless she turned up again the next
day, and Simone, torn between indignation and a curiously warm feeling which she knew to be dangerous, said
no more about it. She did, however, think of several
things she was going to say to Angus when he got back!

That night the telephone rang just before she went to
bed.

CHAPTER SIX

IT WAS Julia. 'Sorry to interrupt your holiday,' she said cheerfully, 'but could I plead with you to come back down to Auckland? There's a party to launch the new perfume from De Roque, and it would be great to have you there.'

'Work?'

Julia chuckled. 'Well, just enjoying yourself mainly. Seeing and being seen—you know how it is.'

Yes, Simone knew how it was, but she most emphatically didn't want to go. Such parties bored her. Seizing on the only excuse that came to mind, she said, 'I haven't brought anything to wear.'

'Never mind about that, I have just the dress for you. It's absolutely beautiful, guaranteed to get you into all the glossies. I'll organise it all.'

'Yes, but——' Simone searched for some other reason to stay at Wainui.

Julia interrupted with an arch little laugh. 'Now don't worry about it, I'll have everything ready for you. We'll put you up at the Pan-Pacific, which is where the "do" is being held, and of course we'll pay your fares back and forth. When can you get down?'

Capitulating to the inevitable, Simone caught back a sigh. 'When is it?'

'Tomorrow night.'

'OK, I'll catch the afternoon plane down from Kerikeri.' No problems there, although Angus would still be away; she'd have to leave Sinbad locked in the bach, but the kitten should be fine overnight if she caught the first plane back again in the morning.

'Right.' Julia was almost purring. 'I'll make all the arrangements so all you'll have to do is enjoy yourself.'

113

The arrangements worked well until Julia unveiled the dress Simone was to wear that evening. It was absolutely beautiful, a romantic fantasy, sand-coloured, high-necked and long-sleeved, strewn with silver and gold lamé roses worked into the mousseline. A wide satin ribbon emphasised Simone's narrow waist, above a full, fairy-tale skirt. Julia had organised shoes of exactly the same colour, and three magnificent ropes of pearls. Exquisite, a dream of a dress, there was only one thing wrong with it; the roses were all that came between her breasts and the gaze of any onlooker.

'No,' Simone said bluntly. 'I'm not going down there half-naked. I'm not wearing it unless I have a camisole.'

'But it will spoil the line,' Julia snapped. 'You could probably get away with it if it didn't have those long sleeves, but a teddy will ruin it.' Her fingers twitched at the transparent sleeves. 'It's meant to be worn like that, for heaven's sake!'

Simone met her frown with a straight, uncompromising look. 'Sorry, but no. You should have known better, Julia.'

'Why the fuss? You'd wear it for a shoot.'

Nodding, Simone said firmly, 'That is different, and you know it.'

Julia snorted. 'How is it different? More people are going to see you in a magazine than there will be at this party!'

'Most of those people reading the magazine will be women. I'm sorry, Julia, but I don't feel comfortable in it.'

Intense exasperation hardened Julia's tone. 'Look, you've made a fortune showing off your body for the last ten years. Why the sudden attack of prudery? I've seen you strip off with photographers around, and never turn a hair.'

'They're accustomed to it, and don't think anything of it. I don't like men ogling me, and you must admit——' one finger touched the golden rose that just covered one soft nipple '—that's what this dress is for, to attract ogling eyes.'

'Oh, for God's sake, Simone! It's not some leather and chain outfit, made to appeal to perverts, or even crudely seductive, all tight and red and strapless! It's soft and romantic and pretty, and the barely covered look is going to be all the rage this winter. If you'd been working the collections in Paris this year you'd have worn a score of dresses like this and never batted an eyelid. Why go all squeamish now?'

Simone began to get out of the beautiful thing. 'Because it's the sort of dress you wear for your lover, on an intimate evening at home, not where every Tom, Dick and Harry can get their kicks working out how to make you laugh so that they can get a glimpse of nipple!'

Her flat conviction must have convinced Julia, for after a tense moment she said crossly, 'Have you got a teddy that'll do the job?'

Of course she hadn't. She had taken Julia at her word and arrived with only one change of clothes, neither of which had any need for a teddy or even a petticoat.

'I have a bra,' she said, and put it on.

But even she had to admit that her plain sports bra ruined the line, and worse, drew even more attention to the soft transparence of the material.

'Well, that's it,' Julia said, not without a note of satisfaction. 'You've arrived so late that all of the shops are closed. You'll have to wear it. Oh, for heaven's sake, Simone,' as Simone opened her mouth to protest further, 'it's not like you to be so coy. Some of those shots of you in bathing suits show damned near as much as this does! You might as well be naked in them—the material reveals almost everything you've got!'

'I do not make a habit of going out in public with everything I've got on display,' Simone said crisply. 'Shots for magazines, even the catwalk, are not the same as deliberately tantalising every man I meet, and you know it.'

Clearly hanging on to her temper with some difficulty, Julia took a deep breath and tried again. 'Look, this is marvellously subtle, it's almost the same colour as your skin; it's only close up that you realise how seductively translucent it is, and in the crush tonight no one's going to be able to see much of you at all.'

'Only my top half,' Simone said grimly, knowing now that she was going to have to wear the exquisite thing or not turn up, and trying to fight off some perception of danger, some foreboding that warned her to stay away, to run back to Wainui as quickly as she could.

Patiently, aware that she had won, Julia coaxed, 'The pearls'll hide anything that needs hiding. Just hold your glass of champagne up in front of you, if you're really that shy.' She smiled, more conciliatory now. 'Look, hop into a robe so they can do your face and hair, and I'll see if I can find something that will do.'

But an hour later, when Simone was waiting with her face made-up, Julia arrived back, spread her hands and said bluntly, 'No, I couldn't find anything, anywhere, that wouldn't look hideous and crass. The dress was made to be worn without underpinnings. And you're not flaunting everything, Simone; those roses are placed in just the right place. You'll look romantic and alluring, that's all. Not in the least cheap.'

Oh, really? Simone thought grimly as she went down in the lift to the ballroom. But Julia had been right; the roses had been placed so cunningly that she was more or less covered. The dress promised a lot, but hid more, in a kind of teasing, demure sensuality that was far more provocative than anything skin-tight and strapless would have been. She would just have to make sure she didn't take a deep breath, or move suddenly.

The party was like all such parties—fun in a superficial way. With a barely touched glass of champagne in her hand Simone circulated, renewing acquaintanceship with people, most of whom she hadn't seen for some time and wouldn't care if she never saw again. But the

De Roque people had done their homework, and the evening possessed glitter and glamour enough to satisfy the most world-weary sophisticate.

Simone parried a few leering comments on her dress with practised ease, noting that there were several every bit as revealing—mostly, she was glad to see, worn by respectable mothers and wives. She laughed, flirted and circulated. She smiled prettily for the photographers, and played her part in the light, sophisticated, almost meaningless conversation that was par for this sort of course. On such occasions people came to display themselves having fun, not to engage in intelligent discussion.

The pearls were useful as armour, but she felt conspicuous even in this worldly crowd, and heartily cursed Julia for getting her into such a situation. Smiling at yet another man, countering his hot gaze and insinuating *double entendre* with a light, frivolous remark, she vowed to make sure it never happened again.

Then she saw a man she recognised, and the mask of sophistication lifted. An imp of mischief, nurtured by the excessive restraint she had been forced to endure all evening, as well as the fact that with Caine Fleming she didn't have to pretend, persuaded her into indiscretion.

'Well, hello,' she breathed into his ear, lowering her lashes to send him a smouldering look that should have scorched his shoes off his feet.

He swung around, laughter narrowing his transparent eyes into wickedness. 'Simone,' he said, and lifted her hand to be kissed with the *savoir vivre* of a man who knew he was very attractive to women. 'Still the same wonderful, gypsyish creature, I see. Are you trying to prove something with that dress?'

'Not a thing. Believe me, this is most emphatically not my idea. I haven't dared breathe all evening. How's Petra?' she murmured, secretly amused by the avid interest they were rousing.

He gave her the smile that had made her heart beat a little faster a year ago when they had first met in San

Francisco, where Caine was the head of an enormous computer firm. Two New Zealanders, aware of an instant liking, they had gone out together a few times. He had taken her to a consulate dinner there, but there had been no question of a romance, even before Simone realised that he was still in love with the wife he had left eight years before.

Now remarried and clearly very happy, Petra and Caine divided their lives between New Zealand and America, where their lovely house was often a stop-over for Simone. After some initial suspicion, entirely understandable on Petra's part, Simone admitted, she and the cool, intelligent, elegant woman who had Caine's heart in thrall had become close friends.

'She's fine.'

'Is she here?'

He grinned. 'No. And I'm not going to be here for long, either. Why don't you come to see her tomorrow morning?'

'I'd love to but I've got a baby to care for.' She explained about Sinbad, joining him in laughter when she had finished.

'Motherhood must be in the air,' he said quietly, his hard mouth softening in the way it did only when he was thinking of his wife. 'Perhaps it's because it's spring. Petra's pregnant. That's why she isn't here tonight.'

Simone felt a sudden pang of envy, but hid it, gazing soulfully up at him with smoky eyes, mischief lurking so deeply in them that only he saw it.

'Lucky woman,' she murmured. 'Tell her I'm green with envy, and that I'll call in and see her when I come back down from my hideaway up north, will you?'

'She'd like that. She's feeling a little fragile at the moment, which is why she's not here tonight. Is there any reason why I'm being subjected to this barrage of high-voltage come-hither? I'm appreciating it immensely, of course; it can only redound to my credit, but you're not normally so—indiscreet.'

'I suppose I'm angry,' she said, remorseful now that she had got over the anger and humiliation she'd been forced to subdue all evening. Feeling cheap and stupid, she dropped her vamp act immediately.

Caine looked at her with perceptive eyes as she explained. 'Hm,' he said when she finished. 'Yes, I see. Why didn't you just refuse to come?'

'Well, they'd paid for me to come down, and oh, well, I owed it to them. I feature largely in the next issue of the magazine.'

'That over-developed sense of responsibility will get you into trouble some day.'

She shrugged, feeling a couple of inches high. 'I'm sorry. I presumed too much on your friendship,' she said on a sigh.

'Don't be silly. There can be no presumption between good friends.'

She looked at him with real affection. 'You're a darling, Caine.'

He grinned. 'So Petra tells me frequently.'

They talked of small things until he finally said, 'I'll have to go. Take care, Simone. You're looking very radiant tonight.' She said nothing but when a wash of purest apricot stole along her cheeks he chuckled, and comprehension warmed his cool, crystalline gaze. 'Oho, so that's what's been happening to you! Who is he? Do we know him?'

'No! Nobody,' she answered, sliding a hunted look sideways through her lashes in case anyone was listening. Fortunately, although they were the centre of attention, no one was near enough to be able to hear what they were saying. 'He's not—I mean, there isn't anybody. Yet.'

Caine laughed deep in his throat. 'How the mighty are fallen! Bring him along so we can vet him.'

But Simone shook her head at him. 'No, I don't know—that is, he doesn't know yet.'

'Poor man.' Caine was still laughing. He made no attempt to hide it, not even when Simone stared at him with irritation. 'I'll bet he doesn't know what's hit him. Well, I want to meet him, and so will Petra, just to make sure he's good enough for you.'

'As soon as anything's settled I'll let you know,' she promised, regaining a little of her composure with a great deal of difficulty. 'If anything ever is settled, that is.'

She smiled pleadingly up at him, willing him not to pursue the subject, and Caine, who was perceptive as well as attractive, grinned and bent to kiss her cheek. 'OK,' he murmured, for her ears alone, 'but Petra and I will be expecting to see you when you get back from this holiday. And I'll bet Petra will get it all out of you!'

Blushing, she laughed and nodded, then froze, her eyes caught by a harshly masculine profile only a few feet away.

'What's the matter?' Caine demanded.

She shook her head, more to clear it than in negation, but it *was* Angus, and as though the agitated swirl of her brilliant hair caught his attention he turned and looked straight at her with a dark, opaque gaze that told her nothing. After a moment his eyes disengaged from hers, and fell to the sheer, revealing bodice of the dress.

Shamefully, her first impulse was to cover her breasts with her hands, but she retained enough self-control not to do that, although that quick, impassive survey scorched into her flesh. It took her a considerable amount of will-power to summon enough poise to smile as he came up, the crowd parting before him like waves before a liner.

She even managed to introduce them, smiling while they exchanged greetings, aloof on Angus's part, a little constrained on Caine's as his eyes slid from her calm face to the harshly sculpted angles and planes of Angus's countenance, disciplined into detachment yet with a hint of strong emotion beneath the sardonic mask.

Fond though she was of him, Simone breathed a sigh of relief when Caine finally left. 'I didn't know you were coming to this,' she said quickly to Angus, striving to hide an entirely unreasonable hurt that he hadn't told her.

He looked down at her, his gaze roaming for a searing few seconds across the glittering flowers and soft translucent fabric that were all that stood between her and nakedness. 'Julia invited me,' he told her aloofly. 'She thought I might find it amusing.' His tone invested the word with contempt.

Some contrary impulse made Simone lift her brows, delicately mocking him. 'I gather you're not enjoying it?'

'Not much,' he said, looking around him with an expression that could only be construed as indifference. 'This is not my sort of scene, but clearly you fit in very well.'

She shrugged, made uneasy by the aura of tightly leashed intensity that crackled around him like St Elmo's Fire. 'It's a business affair,' she explained, 'masquerading as a party. Usually they're quite fun, if you don't expect too much of them. But they're no place for anything but frivolity.' The need to attack rather than defend drove her to look him over, openly appreciating the magnificent sight he made in his well-tailored dinner-jacket. 'And you don't seem at all out of place,' she murmured boldly.

He lifted his brows at that, something ugly gleaming beneath the sweep of his lashes.

Smiling, she leaned closer, dropping her voice so that he had to bend his head to hear it. 'You look superb,' she said, her voice husky, touching her finger to the lapel of his jacket. 'Tall and lean and dangerous, like a very well-dressed pirate.'

He showed his teeth in what was certainly not a smile. 'Whereas you, as I'm sure you know, look like something extremely expensive and very, very good at your job.'

The offensiveness of the *double entendre* drove the colour from her cheeks. Stepping back, she stared up into a face that was hewn from merciless metal, cold and hard and contemptuous. After a moment she turned her head away and said in a stifled voice, 'I can't believe I heard that!'

'Surely you've been parrying remarks like it all evening.'

There was just enough truth in this to make her bite her lip. She looked up, but apart from the glitter in his eyes there was no sign of emotion in his expression. Pride lifted her head. She said between her teeth, 'Not expressed with such crudity, believe me.'

'If it's sophisticated repartee you want,' he returned insultingly, 'you chose the wrong man, Simone. I have no talent for insinuation.'

'Only for jumping to conclusions!'

'Jumping?' He let his half-closed eyes run slowly down the transparent bodice of the dress, lingering on the rose that barely covered each tender aureole. 'There was no jumping, I assure you. You look exquisite, as I'm sure your mirror told you, ravishingly beautiful, and—definitely available. Are you out prospecting, Simone? Because if you're not you're laying yourself open to all sorts of wrong assumptions. And as you're too intelligent not to know exactly what you're doing I can only assume that you're looking for a man tonight. I wish you luck.'

At the beginning, colour had surged from her breasts to her forehead, but by the time he had finished it had fled, leaving her cold and sick.

'You have a vulgar mind,' she said icily.

He smiled that smile that was not a smile, but before he could say anything more a man she barely knew, although she had once rebuffed an open, crude prop-

osition from him, stopped beside them and nodded at
Angus, who inclined his head curtly.

'Hello, Simone,' the intruder murmured with a distasteful leer. 'You're looking very nice tonight.'

She knew how to deal with this sort of thing—a wintry
smile, an aloof thanks, and a quick retreat; but retreat
was impossible.

'Thank you,' she said with a smile that bore more than
a tinge of frost.

Colour scorched in ugly patches over the intruder's
cheeks. 'Although I prefer to remember you as you were
the last night we spent together,' he said, lying by
insinuation.

'On your way.' Angus's voice was cold, bone-chilling,
hard as ice-hewn stone.

'Oh, sorry,' the man said, stepping back in elaborate
withdrawal. But however hard he tried to hide it, it was
involuntary fear that showed in his expression. After a
moment he looked from Angus to Simone, and repeated
nastily, 'Sorry,' before he disappeared.

Julia's voice interrupted them. 'Ah, there you are,'
she said, smiling at them both with an impartiality
Simone only had to look into her eyes to negate. 'Simone,
be careful of that dress, dear, it cost a fortune. I'm so
glad you decided not to wear anything under it; it really
would have ruined it. As it is, you look absolutely superb.
Doesn't she look stunning, Angus?' She tilted her head
on one side, looking Simone over with an intensity that
persuaded Angus to follow suit.

Cold chills ran down Simone's spine. She didn't know
what was going on here, but she didn't like Julia's be-
haviour. Then she looked up into Angus's face, and the
breath stopped in her throat. From beneath those amazingly curled lashes he was looking at her with a contemptuous savagery that lit his eyes with cold blue flames.

'Don't you think so?' Julia persisted, smiling archly
at him.

'Magnificent,' he said tonelessly. 'Like every man's erotic fantasy come true.'

Julia's smile slipped sideways. Simone was a little sorry for her, but not much, because it was slowly becoming clear to her that possibly this whole evening, but certainly Julia's choice of the dress, was a set-up. For some reason not too hard to discern, Julia had chosen this dress in the expectations of just such a reaction from Angus.

'Good,' Simone said crisply, striving to conquer the slow burn of humiliation deep inside her. 'That was, I assume, the object of the exercise.'

Her head was held high, her face blazing with anger. Her glance, sharp as a whetted blade of palest greenstone, sliced into the older woman.

'Exactly,' Julia said a little nervously.

Simone's gaze swung to Angus. He was looking bored, as though he couldn't care less what she thought of him. Pain sawed through her.

She felt degraded, both by wearing the dress and by allowing her worry about Angus's opinion to spin her into this quarrel. He had no right to judge her, no right to look at her as though she were a slut.

Her lashes drooped. She took a deep breath, then flushed as she saw Angus lift his brows. But the pride and self-respect she had worked so hard to acquire came to her rescue.

She smiled, and said lightly, 'It's certainly a lovely dress.'

And then heard Caine's voice from behind, a hard note in it as he said calmly, 'Come and dance with me, Simone.'

Curiosity and wild surmise flashed across Julia's face, were fought back as she beamed at them both. It was impossible to tell what Angus was thinking, but after that last rebuff Simone was ready to go. Her smile had a glittering edge to it, but she said merely, 'Yes, of course,' and walked with him through the crowd to the dance-floor.

'Trouble?' Caine asked after several steps.

She flushed. He was too sharp not to have noticed. 'Nothing I can't handle,' she said frankly, 'but thanks for rescuing me.'

'You can certainly pick them,' he said, reinforcing her knowledge of his acuteness. 'I'm surprised he let you wear that dress.'

She fired up nicely, shooting a furious look upwards. 'He had no say in the matter.'

'He'd like to.' His hand slid up to massage the tight muscles behind her neck. 'Come on,' he coaxed, 'tell me what the trouble is.'

He was very dear, but she couldn't tell him. She shook her head and said softly, 'Someone is going to tell Petra that we were flirting together. I know I started it, and I'm sorry, it was thoughtless of me, but do you think it's a good idea to keep going?'

His face hardened forbiddingly. 'Petra knows she doesn't have to worry,' he said with a cool assurance.

Simone bit her lip. 'I know. It's just that——'

'That you don't want Angus Grey to see you in any sort of compromising situation?'

'I don't care how he sees me,' she said flatly. 'He's a prudish, stuffy——'

'So he did object.' Caine gave a lop-sided grin. 'Any man who wanted you for himself would, Simone. It's a dress made for a woman to wear for her lover when she's alone with him on an evening that's going to have only one ending.'

His remarks were so in accordance with her own views that she sighed. 'I know, but—but he has no right to look at me as though I were something slimy from under a stone.'

Caine laughed softly, without humour. 'Men in the throes of love,' he observed drily, 'are not often very logical, or sensible, and the question of rights seems to go out the window. I'd be furious with Petra if she wore a dress like that for anyone else's eyes but mine.'

'Petra is so dignified she'd probably never allow herself to get into a situation like this. And he's certainly not "in the throes of love".' The heavy sarcasm in Simone's voice hid bleak heartbreak. Her gaze dragged inevitably to Angus's broad shoulders and lean, dangerous maleness as he bent his head to talk to Julia.

'Come on, now, where's your spirit?' Caine held her away for a moment, his shrewd gaze noting the fine tremble of her lips. 'Let's go,' he said abruptly. 'This is no fun for you, and I want to get home too. Where are you staying?'

'Here.' She let him escort her off the floor, suddenly exhausted, her bones so heavy that she leaned gratefully on his strong arm.

Ignoring anyone else, she even acquiesced when Caine insisted on going into the lift with her. At her door she said lightly, 'Thanks. Tell Petra she's got a man in a million.'

He chuckled. 'She knows that. Cheer up, my dear, things will look better in the morning; they always do.'

'Of course,' she said politely, smiling as she closed the door behind him.

But once he was gone the smile faded, leaving her expression turbulent. How dared Angus behave like that? Standing tensely in the luxurious room, she hated him, hated Julia, who clearly had her own agenda in all this, and despised herself for being so stupidly manipulated into such a position. She felt unclean, as though all the leering eyes had left a smutty trail across her skin.

With less than her usual grace she stripped off the beautiful, scandalous dress, and hung it carefully, then creamed the cosmetics from her face, working with an absent-minded skill as she cleaned off every vestige of Trish's painstaking artistry. This time next year, she promised herself, she'd go for weeks at a time with no make-up but moisturiser.

Then, mutinous, muttering, still feeling smirched by the imprint of men's fantasies, still furious at her own bad judgement, she showered long and vigorously, trying to wash off the evening. At last, when the pale ivory of her skin was flushed with rose, she got out and dried herself down before sliding into the towelling bathrobe. The hairdrier took care of her long tresses. When they were free from moisture she leaned forward from the waist, brushing the crackling, blazing skeins of fire with a skilled, careful hand, slowly feeling her emotions calm as the long, soothing strokes straightened and burnished her hair.

And then she stood for a long time with all the lights out, looking down through her window at the lights of the city.

She had been an idiot.

She should have flatly refused to wear that dress. But Angus had no right to call her a slut. Surely these last two weeks had shown him that she was not the sort of woman who went out of her way to be provocative! Her temper simmered as she recalled his crude, brutal words. How dared he?

Unclenching tense fingers from the belt about her waist, she wondered whether she should give up, whether it was useless to hope. Perhaps she should collect Sinbad and go somewhere else for the rest of her month. But Simone didn't give up easily, and when she thought of leaving Angus something in her heart broke softly.

It wasn't just that potent masculine magnetism that attracted her; oh, she wanted Angus Grey with every fibre of her being, so much that at times it was like an aching hunger eating into her, but it was not purely or even mostly physical. In him she found what she thought she'd found with Jason—a true communion.

He could be an arrogant swine, but something in his mind called to her, something stark and subtle and intriguing. He didn't bore her; he made her think, justify ideas and prejudices with a rigorous discipline.

She had been wrong about Jason; was she wrong now, too? She looked down at her fingers, superbly manicured and polished, the hand of a woman who did no physical labour but the exercise needed to keep her pampered body in shape. A thin thread of excitement needled through her as she thought of Angus's lean hands with their calluses, their strength.

He had behaved incredibly badly, but was that jealousy?

Was it some quirk in her character that led to this attraction to men with deep secrets in their hearts? But Angus was not twisted, as Jason had been.

And how do you know? she scoffed as she drew the curtains. He has depths you have never achieved, secrets you have never even guessed at, hidden territories of the mind and emotions you have never been allowed to see.

He wanted her, he enjoyed talking to her; she thought he had liked her. Certainly his laughter had become far more spontaneous than it was two weeks ago, and whenever he had looked at her she had seen a warmth in his expression that was not the cold glitter of lust, or even the shimmering heat of desire. Considering the situation with dispassionate logic, she was certain he had enjoyed the hours they had spent together as much as she had.

Yes, he had liked her. As she had liked him. Until tonight. Did she love him? Did her anger, this feeling of betrayal, hurt so much because she loved him? She crawled into bed, her eyes wide open as she stared at the ceiling, trying to categorise feelings she had until now taken for granted.

What was love? Was it the wildfire hunger that ate at her integrity and her self-respect, combined with the tender warmth that swamped her sometimes when she looked at him? She had thought she loved Jason, but that had turned out to be desire mixed with a childish, preening pride because such a brilliant, famous artist had sought her out. She had been punished for her mistake.

But Angus was a much tougher character than Jason; he would not have shored up his problems with an elaborate and painful set of justifications because he was too afraid to confront them.

No, she thought with a wry smile, Angus was quite capable of hurting himself and everyone else around him, but he would face facts, not hide from them. He had a hard integrity that might wound but at least cut cleanly.

He was going to have to justify his contempt of that evening. She would explain what had happened; if he still thought of her as a slut, well, she thought, bolstering her courage, she'd have to face the fact that she'd made another mistake about a man's character, and cut her losses.

It was only then that she realised just how much it would hurt to turn her back on him and walk away. But Simone had grown up in the years since she had married Jason, developed a strength of mind that would make sure she never again opened herself to such bitter pain and betrayal. Better to make an end of it now than hope to change him, hope that she had been mistaken, and hurt herself so much more when she faced the truth, as she would have to, inevitably.

She would make him listen to her!

It was on this thought that she slept, to wake in the morning to a brilliant, clear dawn—the sort of morning New Zealand did so well. Uplifted, her spirits buoyant, Simone caught the early plane determined to have it out with Angus.

Sinbad was delighted to see her, even climbing up into her lap as she worked on her book. Unfortunately the day deteriorated very quickly so that by the time she drank a cup of tea at four o'clock the weather was turbulent, with rain slashing across the bay and wind rising to shrieking intensity in the gusts. Sinbad demanded to go out into the turmoil shortly after Simone resumed work.

'Well, all right,' Simone grumbled, propping the door open. 'But remember, it was this sort of weather that carried you off before, so take care.'

Two hours later she stretched and stood up, switching the computer off before she went out into the kitchen. Just in case Angus had come she leaned out of the window, but there was no sign of the Range Rover.

Her exhilaration, the confidence of the morning, had gone. Wondering drearily whether he had spent the night with Julia, she stared out into the wild evening.

No, she thought, I *won't* sigh over him like a Victorian maiden! And she went across to begin preparing dinner. The saucer was empty, so she washed it and poured a little more milk into it, then called, 'Puss, puss, puss.'

Normally this brought Sinbad racing eagerly in, but no small marmalade kitten came hurtling across the floor.

'Sinbad! Come on, puss, it's dinnertime.'

But Sinbad didn't appear. Frowning, Simone went into the bedroom, expecting to see a tiny bump under the duvet, but there was no sign of her. At last she went out into the rain, calling.

To no avail. Sinbad didn't appear then, nor at any time in the slow evening as it dragged by. Leaving the back door propped open, Simone finally went to bed at midnight, unable to sleep between worrying about the kitten, and whether Angus and Julia were lovers. An hour later, as she lay restlessly listening to the wind and the rain, she heard the Range Rover come into the garage.

She was horrified by the relief that flowed through her. It seemed to indicate some deeper emotion than the ones she was prepared to admit to—an escalation of emotion from desire and liking to dependence. She had vowed never to let herself become dependent on a man again.

As she lay tossing she heard above the noise of the weather Angus's voice from the back door. 'Simone!' he shouted, coming in with giant strides.

She leapt out of bed, her heart in her mouth. 'Yes, what is it?'

His hands clenched on to her shoulders. He smelled of rain. 'Are you all right?'

'Yes. Yes, of course I'm all right.'

Her astonishment showed in her voice, for he said fiercely, 'I saw that the door was open and I thought of the man who watched us with the binoculars—and the accident——'

'Oh, no!' She swayed towards him. 'No, Sinbad's missing, out in this somewhere, so I left the door open in case she came back home.'

His arms contracted around her in a ferocious embrace. She lay against him, feeling the quick, sharp beating of his heart, smelling the heated, salty scent of him.

Too soon he let her go, putting her away. 'If she's out in this,' he said curtly, 'she'll have found shelter. Lock your door.'

She bit her lip, but obeyed him and made her slow way back to bed. Another gust of rain and wind hurtled against the windows, and she shivered, thinking of her gallant, tough little kitten out in this maelstrom of rain and wind.

Another hammering on the door brought her to her feet and out to the back door. Again it was Angus, but this time he held a small, yawning, somewhat cross but definitely dry Sinbad.

'Oh, thank heavens! Where was she?' Simone reached out, but the wriggling kitten indicated her desire to get down. Once on the floor she ran across to the bowl of milk beside the fridge.

'She was tucked in behind the wood-pile in the garage,' Angus said, looking at Simone with an odd, still watchfulness that made her take an involuntary step backwards.

'Good,' she responded inanely.

He smiled, a narrow, dangerous movement of his lips that intimidated her even more. 'Did you have a good night last night?' he asked, the softness of his voice belied entirely by the raw note embedded in it.

'It was all right.' She was defensive.

'Only all right?' His winged brows rose in mocking query.

Prickles of sensation ran like ants beneath Simone's skin. 'I'm not particularly fond of parties like that,' she said evasively, hiding her unease with an erect head. She was not going to admit that the ugly little scene with him had ruined the whole evening for her.

'Ah, the party. How about afterwards?'

She frowned. 'Perhaps,' she said forthrightly, 'you should tell me exactly what you mean by that.'

'Certainly. The fact that you left the party with your lover did not go unnoticed. Even if I hadn't seen for myself, Julia was careful to point it out.'

Her eyes narrowed. 'I see,' she said starkly, because if she let any emotion into her voice she would explode with fury and despair. So much for all her hopes! 'Caine Fleming happens to be married.'

'I know, but if it doesn't worry him why should it concern you?'

Something broke inside her. 'Why indeed?' she spat, showing her teeth. 'As it happens, however, Caine and I are friends, not lovers. I am also very friendly with his wife. I would find it difficult to be so if I were sleeping with her husband, I can assure you. Petra is an extremely intelligent woman, and she loves her husband enough to trust him, while he worships the ground she walks on. Now get out of here and take your filthy, slimy assumptions with you!'

CHAPTER SEVEN

SIMONE wasn't able to sleep at all that night, and thought it appropriate that morning came sullenly, accompanied by rain and a cold wind from the south.

As she tossed in bed she thought wearily that she hadn't been so shattered since Jason had refused to consummate their marriage.

Well, that showed her how little Angus thought of her. Molten anger fountained through her, but she forced it back under control. She would not let him know how much his sneering insinuations had hurt.

When morning finally made its reluctant appearance Sinbad did her best to charm her from her black mood; the kitten was in a fey mood, darting and pouncing at anything that looked as though it might have any sort of movement in it, her mismatched eyes blazing.

'I wish I had your energy,' Simone told her grumpily as she crawled out of bed.

She showered and dressed, and forced down a cup of coffee and a slice of toast, preparing herself to carry through the decisions she had come to in the forlorn watches of the night. Damn it, Angus was not going to get away with insulting her! Before the day was over he was going to admit that she wasn't the sort of woman to sleep with another woman's husband! It was vitally important that he know, not just in his head, but in his heart.

Face set firmly in an expression her agent would have recognised with a sinking heart, she went out, carefully shutting Sinbad in. Head held so high that it hurt her neck, she marched along to the next unit.

A quick glance through the window revealed that Angus was lying on his side on the floor, propped up on one elbow amid a collection of papers, dark brows drawn together in a frown of complete concentration. As she watched, he put the paper down on one pile, and picked up a fresh one from the other. He wore faded jeans that outlined his thighs with loving precision.

That was all. Above the waistband of the jeans his magnificent chest and shoulders were bare, the muscles moving sleekly beneath bronzed skin that glowed with the healthy sheen of a well-fed beast. Not, Simone thought, standing stock still, that there was anything too well fed about Angus. Raw power shone darkly from him, an animal strength that owed nothing to centuries of civilisation, everything to genes that had fashioned man to be a predator. He was magnificent.

Swallowing to ease the sudden dryness in her throat, she moved past the window. Even then his image was imprinted on her brain. She forced herself to draw several deep breaths before she knocked.

When he opened it he had a shirt on, obviously dragged on in a hurry as it was still unbuttoned down the front. He looked at her with eyes as dark and impenetrable as the winter sea.

'I did not sleep with Caine Fleming,' she said baldly, her tones belligerent.

He lifted a brow, but held open the door, saying without emotion, 'Come inside.'

It was warm inside, too warm. No wonder, she thought hollowly, he had taken off his shirt. 'Well?' she demanded, coming to a stop in the middle of the room.

The corner of his mouth quirked. If she hadn't known better she might have thought him amused. 'All right,' he said matter-of-factly.

She knew her mouth had dropped open, and had to close it with a snap. 'Just like that?' she asked incredulously. 'You make the filthiest insinuations about me and then admit you were wrong?'

'Would you prefer I defend my filthy insinuations?'
'*No!*'

He grinned, devastatingly. 'Poor Simone,' he taunted.
'You came in aflame with righteous indignation, and I've
taken the wind out of your sales completely. Do you
want an apology?'

'It would help,' she said stiffly.

His smile was lop-sided but he said, 'I'm sorry. Put
it down to—a vulgar mind, didn't you call it? That and
the fact that your name had been linked with his—and
a certain jealousy—made me jump to an unforgivable
conclusion.'

She bit her lip, warmed a little by the thought of him
being jealous, yet unable to shake the thought that he
was laughing at her. 'All right,' she said ungraciously,
and turned to go.

He detained her with a hand on her arm. 'Drink a
peace cup of coffee with me?' he suggested smoothly.

'Aren't you busy?'

He cast an irritated glance at the two neat piles of
paper on the floor. 'No, I've been working too long. I
need time to assimilate it.'

She shouldn't, but when he looked at her with that
half-smile, disturbingly sensual yet free from intimi-
dation, she couldn't resist. The righteous anger that had
kept her awake all night seeped away so fast that she felt
slightly ashamed of herself. 'OK,' she said gruffly.

Ten minutes later she was sitting stiffly on a chair,
drinking his excellent coffee. He had picked up the piles
of papers, and buttoned up his shirt. Not that it made
any difference. Simone could see him in her mind,
sprawled like a great lazy cat on the floor, relaxed, yet
with the uncanny alertness that marked all predators.

The image made her jumpy, her instincts at war with
caution, reluctantly admitting the allure of that leashed
sensuality. It was ironic that she, who had posed near
enough to naked with some of the world's most
handsome men, should want so badly a man whose fea-

tures, though striking, were not exactly handsome. But Angus possessed something that none of those models had—a natural, unforced sexuality that indicated a man with the subtlety and power to take a woman to heaven in his arms.

'You're looking thoughtful,' he observed as he handed over a mug of coffee.

She shrugged. 'Rain makes me pensive.'

'Perhaps you should have gone somewhere tropical for this holiday. Northland in spring can have plenty of rain.'

She shrugged. 'Summer is the usual rainy season in the tropics, so I'd get rain wherever I went, unless it was the Atacama desert in South America, where, I believe, it hasn't rained for the last twenty years. I don't mind being pensive now and then.'

He grinned, and cocked a brow at her. The silence while they drank their coffee was companionable, almost restful, in spite of the narrow net of tension that stretched invisibly between them whenever they were in the same room.

Or within ten feet of each other, Simone thought savagely, wondering why she should be so attracted to a man who clearly would take whatever she offered, but had no intention of offering anything of himself.

And it had become borne in on her last night that she wanted much more than sex from him. Oh, it would be wonderful, no doubt about it. Her eyes drifted along the emphatic statement of his shoulders, broad enough to shut out the world, the deep masculine triangle of chest and rib-cage, and the narrow waist above long, strong thighs. Yes, she could lose her soul in his embrace, in his bed.

But he wouldn't. If they made love there would be nothing soulful about it for him. All she would get of him would be brilliant physical satisfaction. She was greedy, she wanted so much more than the pleasure of his body. She wanted all of him.

Because she had fallen in love with him.

'That,' he stated, removing the empty coffee-mug from her hand, 'is a very strange look.'

She said nothing, her eyes smoky and dazed as she looked up into his face. At that moment, shocked by the discovery of her own emotions, she could only stare while her brain tried to grapple with this revelation.

'Simone,' he said, his voice amused yet with a deep note to it that brought her to her senses.

How much had she given away? Everything?

He pulled her up from the comfortable old chair and into his arms as though she belonged there, and tipped her chin with his thumb, holding her exposed to his merciless gaze. His eyes were lit from within by a fierce blue flame that scorched through the defences she was trying so hard to re-erect.

'Witch,' he murmured, 'with your slanting green eyes and that passionate, wilful mouth, and that taunting, laughing sensuality—I've been wanting you for weeks, it seems, for years—for long before I ever met you. And now I have you as spellbound as I am...'

It was too late, too late. Simone watched his mouth come closer, her lashes fluttering down at the last moment so that she couldn't see the feral triumph glittering in his eyes. She expected a fierce kiss, but his mouth was warm and gentle, oh, subtle, as sweet as run honey... Surely he had to feel more than passion for her?

It was her last coherent thought. Like a magician he summoned the deeply sensual woman who had hidden behind the glossy mask of the model, the woman who had been prevented by a sick husband and her own fears from satisfying her deepest desires. His mouth was like wine, tempting, intoxicating, dangerous. Simone let herself be gathered closely against him. His masculine scent tormented her nostrils, the heat from his body enveloped her.

He lifted his head and she sighed, turning her face to kiss the whispery line of his cleft chin, the corners of that wide, firm mouth, the pulse that throbbed like a runaway metronome in his throat.

'Sweet,' he said in a voice she barely recognised. 'So sweet...'

His mouth took toll again, but this time there was more than the slow seduction of that first kiss; this time he made himself master of her response, coaxing her lips open, exploring deeply, purposefully, while her heart threatened to burst through the confines of her body.

Somehow she managed to wrench open the buttons of his shirt, and she touched him at last, her sensitive fingertips smoothing across the expanse of his chest, feeling the rise and fall as he breathed, the abrasive contrast of the dark whorls of hair against the heated satin of his skin, that infinitely alluring fragrance, pure male, slightly salty, a hint of musk; the promise of sex.

When he released her mouth she turned her face into his chest, rubbing her cheeks against the iron muscles with a slow, sinuous appreciation, touching him with little catlike dabs of her tongue, tasting the male essence of him.

He muttered something and lifted her, the muscles in his arms bulging as he clamped her against him, his face buried between her breasts. Simone slid her fingers through the thick bronze silk of his hair, down to the back of his neck, along to the soft, vulnerable hollows beneath his ears, discovering the infinite attraction of his skin, the stark strength of his jaw, its muscles knotted as though he was striving to control an emotion that was uncontrollable.

The heat of his breath scorched through her shirt to her skin, sensitising it, sending sensuous little shudders all the way through her body.

A blind, meaningless smile curled her mouth. Yes, he had to feel something more for her than a mindless lust, or he wouldn't be so determined not to let his passion run away from him.

Then he slid her down the length of his body and she gasped, for there was no doubt that he was aroused. The hard strength of his body told her even before she felt the unmistakable physical signs of his hunger.

For a second her gaze flew up, shock and something perilously like fear in it, and he smiled and said, 'When the time comes you'll take me, I promise, Simone; we'll fit together like hand and glove, like heart and soul.' He bent his head, whispering against her mouth, 'Like need and satiation, like fire and smoke, like hunger and satisfaction, like passion and fulfilment...'

That searing descent down the rigid contours of his body sent tiny flames through her, flames that were blown into an inferno by the deep, husky words of his promise. With a soundless sigh she gave herself to him, surrendering to the need flicking through her like the small, impatient strokes of some celestial whip, moaning softly in the back of her throat as the fires coalesced, setting her whole body aflame, joining at the junction of her body, tightening across her breasts, searing through her when he kissed the long, smooth line of her throat.

Simone had been kissed like this before, touched like this before, but, although Jason used to bare her and caress her, stroke her, delight in cruelly arousing her, he had refused to quench the fires he had roused. Of course, he had been afraid of his impotence, but there had been something cruel and desperate in the way he had caressed her.

She had thought she wanted him; as her fists clenched on to the material of Angus's shirt she realised that she had never before known the meaning of desire, of frustration. 'Please,' she whispered as he slid the buttons of her shirt open, 'oh, please. Yes, Angus, please.'

His hands on her breasts were gentle yet she could feel the restraint he imposed on himself, shiver at the tremor in his fingers as they stroked the soft ivory skin. And she did not want him to be restrained. She was going out of her mind, torn into shreds by the force of this need, and she wanted him to be the same, to be unable to control himself, to be as lost as she was in this new world of the senses.

He was looking at her with total absorption, his dark face drawn and closed apart from the leaping lights in his eyes. She shuddered, for he hadn't touched her nipples, yet they were peaking, the small buds imploring as he cupped the generous weight of her breast, admiring the contrast between his lean dark fingers and the lush richness they cupped.

Her breath blocked her throat. He picked her up and carried her across to the divan, laid her on it and in one swift movement wrenched his shirt free of his body and came down beside her, lowering his head so that he could reach the aching, pleading centre of her breast with his mouth.

A spasm of sensation shot through her. She arched and gave a muffled cry, bewildered yet enraptured at the strange potency of his mouth on her flesh, suckling.

Her hands clenched at her sides; every sinew stiffened almost to pain, and she felt an intolerable aching need suffuse her, pooling hotly in the juncture of her thighs to a hunger at once pain and ecstasy.

He lifted his head, but only a fraction, speaking so that his lips moved against her violently sensitised skin. 'Touch me, Simone.'

Jason had never allowed her to touch him. She had never wanted to touch him as she wanted to touch Angus. Slowly, as though she approached something forbidden and dangerous, she slid her hand across his shoulder, over the flexing muscle, her fingertips skimming across his burning skin with the delicacy of a feather. He was magnificent, all the forbidden dreams in all her nights come true.

That small, sultry smile pulled in the corners of her mouth. It should have straightened the deep indentation in her top lip, but somehow it emphasised it, pulling it into kissing shape. She bent to touch her lips to his shoulder; he tasted of salt and another wild, exotic flavour. Aroused male. Angus. Following an impulse that hadn't been in her brain a millisecond before, she brought her teeth together, nipping him with something more than gentleness.

He laughed deep in his throat. 'Do you like to hurt?' he asked. 'Do you like being hurt? All right, then.'

This time his mouth was not gentle, and she stiffened at the soft scrape of his teeth, but he didn't hurt her, not then, not at any time, so she submitted with that blind siren's smile and went on with her exploration, touching him with wondering delight, tracing the line of his back from shoulder to waist, caressing the hard musculature of his arms, arching without volition as his mouth worked its ancient magic on her breast, on the soft hollow in her throat, on the fragile inner elbow, the wildly sensitive blue veins at her wrist, seductive yet demanding on the fleshy mount beneath her thumb and the palm of her hand.

He had to be incredibly experienced to know just where to touch her. But at that moment she didn't care; her body was all that mattered, and the assuagement of the need he was building so carefully, stoking to a passion that held nothing of logic or reason, nothing but a feral, primitive hunger.

When he opened the waistband of her jeans and slid the zip down she couldn't have stopped him even if she had wanted to. Instead, she mimicked his actions, her hands trembling as she pushed the soft blue cloth free of his hips, all inhibitions gone.

He smiled, a mixture of triumph and satisfaction, and stripped, letting his clothes fall with hers over the side of the divan. For a moment something struggled to make itself heard within Simone's mind, but she banned it from her consciousness, surrendering with wild hunger to the lean, virile potency of his body as he came down beside her.

'You are so unbearably beautiful,' he said softly, running his fingers from the centre of her breast to the dimple of her navel. Her muscles contracted beneath that questing touch, and his teeth showed white as he smiled tigerishly. 'A dream, lush and lovely, all woman, fiery and hot and hungry. Simone...'

He caught her hands, preventing them from conducting their own exploration, and rolled her over on to her back, moving over her with a smooth animal grace that was somehow at odds with the primitive need in his face.

'Give yourself,' he said quietly. 'Give yourself to me, Simone.'

Instinct and the clamouring imperatives of her own body told her what to do. She pulled him down, mouth to mouth, breast to breast, thigh to thigh, and took him into her, gasping at the sudden invasion, the sense of enclosure as he thrust into her. There was a little pain, not much, and after that a galloping pleasure, slow at first, and then hard and fast until the world exploded into shards of fire and she cried out with delight and shock, unaware of his climax until her racing heart eased down and she realised that he was lying in her arms, his chest moving harshly as he gasped for breath.

A warm golden tide of delight rolled through her, leaving her replete, sated with pleasure. This, she thought with a smile that she knew was smug, this was what she had been born for.

Then he said in a voice that for all its silky quietness did not hide the fact that he was furious, 'How is it that you were still a virgin when you've been married?'

Such was her delight that she had forgotten Jason, forgotten everything but her pleasure in Angus. Now, like a dark cloud that never went away, she felt the bleak shadow of that marriage over her again.

'He—I—we didn't ever make love,' she said, the words tripping over her tongue.

'I know that. Now. Why?'

She couldn't tell him; she couldn't explain that Jason hadn't wanted her, that all his emotions, all his passion had been channelled into his paintings, leaving nothing over for the real woman.

'I—we just didn't. And it's not any of your business, is it?' She tried to sound calm and reasonable, but the voice that emerged was husky and defiant.

Lean, strong fingers twisted her face around to meet his merciless, uncompromising stare. She lay very still, pulling the mask of her beauty around her, veiling her eyes into guarded inscrutability.

'It is when I think I'm taking an experienced woman to bed and discover a virgin.'

The strain of meeting that cold and controlled menace was telling; Simone felt the muscles in her neck protest, but her chin remained high, almost arrogant. 'I knew what I was doing,' she said curtly. 'You didn't seduce me.' Colour ran from her breasts to her forehead, staining her skin with a wild, soft apricot. 'I wanted you just as much as you wanted me,' she finished.

'Is that why he committed suicide?' he pressed relentlessly, giving no quarter. 'Because you wouldn't sleep with him?'

She stiffened. 'What?'

'You heard what I said.' Her mouth dropped as he went on calmly, 'Did the poor devil get tired of waiting? I know he wanted you. I've seen one of the paintings he did of you, and the sexuality smouldered through the paint.'

Her colour fled. *'What?'*

'The one of you lying on deep green velvet,' he said slowly, pinning her with the hard hunger of his gaze. 'It was a nude. You were smiling. And believe me, Simone, the man who painted that would have given his soul to take you.'

She couldn't believe it. 'It was burned,' she said desperately. 'They were all burned.'

'Not that one.'

She turned her head, shame and humiliation darkening her eyes. 'I was told they were all destroyed,' she said dully. 'How many others are there?'

'As far as I know that's the only one.'

'Who owns it?'

Something unpleasant moved in his eyes. 'Why?'

But although the shock was still acute she was recovering some of her poise. 'I just want to know,' she said.

'Now, why do I get the idea that you don't like the idea of anyone owning a nude of you?' She knew that those shrewd eyes noted her automatic rigidity. 'Especially when showing that delicious body clearly doesn't worry you at all. If it did, you wouldn't have worn that dress the night before last.'

'Let me go!' she said between gritted teeth, unable to lie exposed before him like this. She pushed, but he held her effortlessly, his expression slightly wolfish, his hands like iron clamps on her arms, the weight of his body stopping her from using her knees to hurt him.

They fought a short, inevitable battle, but it ended with her panting and furious beneath him, forced to endure his weight, angry and shocked when she realised that her struggles were arousing him.

'But then,' he resumed meditatively, watching her with that cold, cold gaze, 'you're not exactly noted for the depth of your emotions, are you? You worked the day after your mother died, for example, instead of going home. Julia showed me the photographs—superb. A lovely, laughing, sensuous woman. No one would ever have known that you were nursing a broken heart.'

It was obvious from his tone that he certainly didn't believe it.

Ice crawled up through her, freezing the joy and delight, the languid, lazy warmth as though it had never existed. She said harshly, 'I'm a professional. It's my job to look like that.'

'Julia said she offered to get another model but you insisted on finishing the shoot.'

Seared by bitter betrayal, Simone stared up at him, hating him. 'Let me go,' she said tightly. 'I don't have to listen to this.'

He hesitated, as though he wanted to insist she answer, then let her free. Moving stiffly, she hauled her clothes on again, keeping her back to him so that he couldn't see her expression. Modesty was forgotten; she wanted only to get out of the room, get out of his life. What had been the most wonderful experience of her life was rapidly turning into a nightmare every bit as bad as the memories of her time with Jason.

He said harshly, 'I suppose you're not even protected.'

'You suppose wrongly.' Her voice was icy, her face immobile as a statue, all the colour fled from her perfect skin so that she looked like an ivory carving. 'You don't need to worry about anything, Angus. As a lover you're very good—no virgin could have asked for a better or more skilful deflowering.'

Her shoulders stayed erect all the way into her unit, all the way into the shower, and only when the taps were turned on and the water drowned out the sound of her tears did she give way to them, weeping softly, heart-brokenly, all the grief she felt for her mother mingled in with the shattering pain of his betrayal.

When she had washed the scent and feel of him from her body she dressed in cords and a medallion-print shirt in her favourite corals and peach tonings, and pulled on a huge, long jersey, for in spite of the heat from the fire she was cold. Sinbad came frolicking across the floor and as Simone's eyes filled again she snatched the little kitten up and buried her face in the fragrant fur.

For once Sinbad did not object. After a while Simone lifted her face and said through gritted teeth, 'He is not

going to get away with this. Damn him, I love him! That
has to mean something!'

Common sense dictated that she give him some time
to simmer down. Although Simone was almost totally
inexperienced when it came to love, she was astute
enough to realise that Angus was as angry with himself
as he was with her, and the reason for that had to be
that he had mistaken her status. Instead of the sophisticated, sensual widow he had assumed her to be, she
had turned out to be a virgin.

Naturally, she thought, trying hard to be worldly, he
was shocked. And angry. It seemed as though he was a
little hung up about being the first man who had taken
her to bed.

And perhaps he despised himself for wanting the sort
of woman he'd so clearly thought she was! A tease,
shallow, easily consoled... How dared he?

She got to her feet and began pacing back and forth,
talking softly to Sinbad. 'He's just shaken, and I suppose
he doesn't want to accept that he's been wrong about
me. Nobody likes feeling a little foolish. When he calms
down I'll tell him about my marriage with Jason.'

A cold shiver ran down her back. Even now it was
hateful for her to remember, but she owed it to him.

'And,' she said, her face setting into severity, 'I'll tell
him that Julia lied. That was a lousy thing to do, Sinbad,
although I suppose I know why she did it. I could tell
she thought he was wonderful. Well, I did myself, even
though I didn't want to admit it! So later this evening,
after I've rung Jason's agent and found out who owns
that awful picture and if there are any others of them
around, when Angus has had time to think a bit, we'll
go over and we'll make him see that he needn't worry
about my lack of experience. I chose him; I could have
stopped him at any time—he's not the sort of man who
would force a woman—but I wanted him every bit as
much as he wanted me.'

The sound of the Range Rover brought her head round. She couldn't see it, as the drive went along the back of the units, but she listened hard to its progress out on to the road.

Uneasiness ate its way through her, but she ignored it. He would be back, and when he was she would be waiting for him.

He didn't come back. Not that day, not the next, not at all. He left a note in the letter-box telling her that he was sorry, he regretted very much what had happened; he had assumed that she was an experienced woman and all he had wanted from her was an affair. If by any chance there was anything she needed to see him about, could she contact him through Julia?

The cold, distant allusion to the possibility of a pregnancy made Simone flinch even more than his allusion to Julia. Like hell would she make any sort of contact with him! She was forced to accept that he wanted nothing more of her.

And eventually, when she went one step further and forced herself to accept that it was for the better, that he was too cold, too locked inside the iron-bound prison of his contempt to be able to give her what she needed from a man, Simone was able to face the fact that she had once more given herself to the wrong man, and was again going to reap the harvest of her own illusions.

Her telephone call to Jason's agent began in bitter acrimony, but he said instantly, 'Simone, that was the only one, I swear it, and it was sold before he k-died.' His memory of the ones she had made him destroy hardened his voice. 'It was a private sale.'

'Who owns it?' She believed him, and her anger died with the hideous prospect of all those others circulating on some sort of black market of connoisseurs.

She could hear his shrug. 'Who knows? I can search through the documents if you really want to know, but six years ago—well, it will take me some time. And that will only tell you who bought it the first time. It could have changed hands a couple of times, you know. Plenty of these high-fliers have come to grief since then.'

'I want to know who owns it,' she said adamantly.

'OK, OK, I'll do it.'

She spent the remaining days at the unit, clawing back some sort of poise and control while her heart felt as though it was breaking, shattering inside into jagged shards.

Working on her manuscript helped. When she was editing she had to concentrate ferociously and was able to lose herself in it for hours at a time. It didn't make her emotions any easier to bear, but at least it gave her some kind of much-needed oblivion.

Finally it was the last day. She packed, and called Sinbad, but the kitten was gone, out in the yard on one of its mysterious missions. Tears burned suddenly in Simone's eyes.

'No,' she said quietly, 'I'm not going to cry. No, no, *no*. Sinbad,' she called. 'Puss, puss, puss, come on, time to go.'

But no small marmalade butterball emerged from around the side of the house—not then, and not the next morning when Simone should have been in Auckland if she was going to catch her plane without undue rush.

She had rung Mrs Jackson the night before, after searching as far afield as she could in the time. The farmer's wife had agreed to leave food out, and, if she could, catch Sinbad and send her on to a cattery.

When she got off the telephone Simone bit her lip, and it was with tears in her heart that she made the final dash down to Auckland, catching her jet to America by the slimmest of margins.

She had been working non-stop for three weeks when she wrote to Mrs Jackson to ask whether Sinbad had ever turned up. Another busy month passed before she got the answer on a grey November day in the form of a note from Mrs Jackson.

Your kitten arrived back two days after you left. Mr Grey said he'd put it in the cattery and took it back to Auckland with him.

He'd come back! Ecstasy whiplashed through her.

But quick as lightning came the realisation that he had known she was leaving on that day; she had made no attempt to hide it. So he had known she wouldn't be there.

Stupid tears sparkled in her eyes, were hastily wiped away with her fingers. Her emotions had been like a seesaw ever since—well, ever since he had gone.

'All eyes,' her agent had said sternly a week before. 'Slim is one thing, honey, scrawny is entirely another. Eat something. And forget the guy. He's not worth it.'

Which was easy enough for her to say; it seemed that Simone was cursed with total recall where Angus was concerned. It was slowly being borne in upon her that she was not going to forget him. She loved him. She wanted him, she needed him, she missed him rather more than she would miss her own heartbeat; she dreamed of him at night and she fantasised about him while she was working, and, although magazine editors and designers and fashion show producers adored the new Simone with the mysterious, almost wistful smile, the pain stayed right in her chest like a large, insurmountable lump. It didn't even go when she signed the contract for her manuscript.

The only relief she could find was when she worked on the second one, using it as a reason for not going out.

CHAPTER EIGHT

AFTER thirteen months' absence, Auckland was the same as ever—enchanting. For one of the American hostesses it was her first flight into the city, and, as the jet came down over the sparkling, exquisite panorama of sea and islands, land and tiny, abrupt volcanoes, she went from side to side of the plane, uttering little cries of pleasure and delight.

Simone's spirits, already heightened, soared. Somewhere down there was Angus. And Sinbad.

Simone had had letters from him over the past year; not much, merely a few casual notes enclosing photographs of the cat, now sleek and fully adult. Each time the distinctive black writing had appeared on an envelope her heart had thumped, but there was never anything personal in them, and none of the photographs showed him. But they were an indication that he didn't want to sever contact completely. And where there was contact, she thought stubbornly, there was hope.

Sometimes she thought she might die of the need to see him again, to hear him speak, to know that he was there. But, as long as his obsession with a physical type prevented him from seeing her as a woman he could love, she knew her love was doomed to be unrequited.

And as far as obsessions went Simone had come to the bitter conclusion that she had to be attracted to men who had that sort of personality!

She hadn't let anyone know that she was coming back, so there were no journalists or photographers waiting. After Customs she came out into the fresh air of a perfect spring day, setting her jaw as she climbed into the taxi. Simone the world-famous super-model no longer existed. Simone Atkinson was beginning her life.

And, she thought with a pang of painful anticipation, the first thing she was going to do was visit her cat.

Angus lived at Pukapuka, an area about forty minutes north of Auckland. His postal address was a box number in Warkworth, a pretty, small town a little further north; he had not given her his proper address on those short letters, so presumably he didn't want her to contact him except through the post. She had had to employ a private detective to discover exactly where he lived. It made her feel sneaking and sly, but it was, she told herself righteously, his own fault.

She wandered across the luxurious room, like so many others she had slept in during the last eleven years, and stood for a long time staring out on to the glittering waters of the harbour.

His rejection had wounded her to the soul, cut into her precious store of self-confidence like a knife through butter, battering her pride and her love into the mud. But she had waited a year for this reckoning, and she wasn't going to wait any longer.

The hotel organised a hire car for her, and a map, although she knew how to get there. Pukapuka was not a town, just a country district set beside an extravagantly beautiful estuary bordered by pale beaches and steep hills. Angus had once said that he would build beside a beach; perhaps this was his dream house.

Carefully, for it had been a year since she had driven on the left, she made her way through Auckland's busy traffic until she got on to the northern motorway. From then it was easy. There wasn't much traffic on the main highway, so although she had to concentrate on the road she was well aware of the brilliant beauty of the day, gold and green, with tantalising glimpses of the sea to the right. It was a month closer to summer than when she had been this way last, and the lambs and calves were just that much bigger. Only a few lingering blooms starred the daffodil clumps in the paddocks, and the cherries were fading, but the flame trees were still brilliant and the first sign of mauve was misting the bare jacaranda branches.

Three quarters of an hour later she turned off to wind her way down the narrow sealed road that dipped and climbed along the southern side of the estuary. The Mahurangi river gleamed like molten silver between its banks of farmland and bush, and the air that came in through her open window was crisp and pure and warm, scented by the sea.

Several minutes later she stopped under the large puriri tree that marked the entrance to Angus's house. For a moment she breathed deeply, fighting to overcome panic. She had planned this meeting for six months, as soon as she was able to register that Angus was not going to relent, and whatever came of it she would not back down now.

Hands careful on the wheel, she turned the car down the steep, narrow track cut around the edge of the hill.

The house was set on its own bay; she could see a red corrugated iron roof set in a tangle of vegetation. It did not look like anyone's dream house. Cautiously, coming once to a halt to miss hitting a sheep and two lambs that hadn't the sense to get off the drive, Simone made her way down and over the cattle-stop.

Silence assailed her ears when she switched off the engine. For a moment she almost switched it straight back on again and drove away, but her chin came up. She stepped out of the car, wiping her wet palms on her trousers.

The house was not new, not even very well kept, and the overgrown garden was a wilderness of old-fashioned shrubs. With anticipation and foreboding warring in her stomach she found her way between the two large camellia trees studded with pink and white blooms, and on past a datura, the scent from its white trumpets sweet and erotic on the air. Then she saw Sinbad, lying watching her with narrowed eyes from the veranda rail, the morning sun turning her fur to gold.

'Hello, Sinbad,' Simone said softly. 'Remember me?'

The cat purred, even allowed Simone to stroke her, but she was clearly not enthralled to see her. There was no recognition at all in the great, mismatched eyes.

For some strange reason it struck Simone like a blow. 'Indifferent, are you?' she said, persevering. 'Like your master, no doubt.'

'What the hell are you doing here?'

Simone's hand stilled in the sun-warmed fur. Carefully she looked up into the shade beneath the veranda roof. Old-fashioned french windows were pushed wide open, and between them, like some grim god of yesteryear, stood Angus.

Her chin jerked up. 'I came to see my cat.' She gave Sinbad a last stroke before walking up the steps on to the wooden veranda.

He looked—just the same. Arrogant, forceful, inflexible; in spite of his greeting there was no surprise, no welcome, no sign of any emotion at all in his countenance.

'Is that all?'

She shrugged and came closer. 'That's up to you.'

The opaque indigo eyes surveyed her with offensive thoroughness from the tip of her head to the toes of her tan loafers. She had dressed very carefully for this, in triple-pleated trousers and a cashmere polo jersey, both camel-coloured, with a wide tan belt emphasising her slender waist. Over her arm was a moss-green trench-coat. Beyond lip-gloss she wore no make-up at all.

'You look very chic,' he commented, his mouth curling on the word. 'Do you feel like roughing it again for a few days, enjoying another roll in the hay with one of the local peasants? How long can you stay this time?'

The insult drove the colour from her skin but she said steadily, 'I don't have to go again. I've given up modelling.'

He lifted that brow, devastating her. 'Have you? If you did it for me, Simone, the sacrifice was in vain. I don't want you here.'

'I didn't do it for you,' she said evenly, refusing to react to that last cold statement. 'I had already made the decision when I met you. As you would have known if you'd given me a chance to tell you instead of running away.'

'Was that how it seemed to you?' He smiled, a cold, humourless movement of his mouth. 'I suppose it was. It appeared to be the easiest way of putting an end to a situation I found intolerable.'

'No doubt you were afraid you might seduce me again,' she agreed in a voice as hard as his. 'I should be grateful for your—discretion, I suppose.'

Something ugly flashed into his expression, was instantly reined back by that formidable will. He said distantly, each word as cold and as hard as a pebble, 'You've come on a wild-goose chase, I'm afraid. I don't need you, I don't want you, I don't even like you. Why don't you get your smooth, elegant, superficial self back into your car and go back to the world you adorn so prettily?'

'Why didn't you tell me that you owned the portrait?' she said hurriedly, because he was going to do it, he was going to throw her out, and she couldn't think of anything else to stop him.

That stopped him. The muscles in his shoulder bulged as though he was clenching his fist, and suddenly this seemed the most foolhardy thing she had ever done.

'How did you find out?' he asked silkily.

Her full mouth twisted. 'You can find out anything if you have the money,' she said. 'But this didn't cost much; it wasn't exactly a secret, was it? Jason's agent told me. It must have been a long, interesting talk you had with Jason when you decided to buy it, Angus. The agent said you bought it because the model looked very like your wife. Are you fixated on that colouring, Angus—red hair and the pale skin and green eyes?'

He was across the boards of the veranda so quickly she didn't have a chance to react before his hands were grasping her upper arms. 'It certainly seems so, doesn't it?' he ground out. 'Fixated on models, on women who need their own fixes of glamour and superficial excitement and money. And the occasional earthy tumble.' He dragged her against him, one lean hand pushing her hips with casual force into his so that she could feel his arousal. 'Is this what you want, Simone? Well, I'm no damned stud, I'm not going to take you to bed just because you've got an itch.'

'How about taking me to bed because I want you?' she asked gravely, trying to keep her voice steady.

He looked down at her with something like fury seething in the black-sapphire depths of his eyes, lips drawn back in a snarl, and then his head swooped and he kissed her, possessing himself of her mouth with such passion that she gasped.

It was the same, yet given a keener edge by the months she had spent away from him, the longing, yes, even the anger and the sense of black betrayal she had endured when she had discovered his reason for buying the portrait. Her mouth responded, her whole body arching with a passionate fire into his, and for the first time in a year she felt the sharp spear of desire, sweet and fiery, a torment and a delight.

The kiss softened, deepened; anger was slowly transmuted to something else, something her body recognised before her brain did. Fire fountained up through her, and she groaned beneath the brand of his mouth, longing for so much more, yet almost content with the taste of him, the subtle scent of aroused male, the silk of his skin beneath her fingers as her hands slid lovingly around his neck.

But at last the kiss ended. She turned her head into his throat, and put her lips to the pulse throbbing there. 'Good God,' he said unevenly into her hair. 'Get the hell out of here, Simone, before I do something you'll never forgive me for.'

'I don't think there's anything you could do that I wouldn't forgive you,' she said softly.

He dragged her back, shaking her until the brilliant flames of her hair fell forward over her face. Then he dropped his hands and stepped back, his lips drawn back from his mouth in a snarl as he swore fluently. She looked fearlessly up into a countenance chiselled into angles by the primal force of his desire.

'I don't want you here,' he said through gritted teeth. 'I don't like what you do to me, what you make me.'

'And what is that?'

'A creature of despicable impulses, uncontrollable urges. I don't love you. I don't feel anything but lust for you. Are you content with that? Is that what you want, to sate your desire with my lust?'

His words cut her heart out, but she said quietly, 'If that's all I can get, then yes, that's what I'll take.' She had known it wasn't going to be easy. Somehow he had convinced himself that loving was a betrayal, that to admit to it again made him a lesser man. She had to convince him that it was not, and she thought she knew how to do it.

And if she was wrong, well, she would have something of him to keep and love. The memories of her brief, sad marriage would be replaced by golden recollections of an honest passion.

His eyes scorched across her face, merciless, probing for some sort of reaction. Simone kept her expression as composed as she could, knowing that if she relaxed her guard he would see through to the riot of emotions inside her.

Tension throbbed between them, tension and a kind of acceptance. 'Are you sure?' he said at last, determined not to make it easy for her.

Elation burst into a million bubbles inside. 'Yes, I'm certain,' she said, trying to hide it, trying to be as matter-of-fact as he was.

'Even though I'm not offering marriage? I'll take you whenever I feel like it and give you nothing?'

It hurt. Pain raked her heart, but she said with a self-derisory smile, 'You'll give me your lovemaking. That's enough.'

'You've nothing to judge it against,' he retorted harshly.

How did he know that he was still the only man she had made love with? She lifted her brows, allowing laughter mixed with mockery to appear in her expression. 'If it was any better I wouldn't know how to cope.'

He gave a thoughtful, unsettling look. 'Then come inside, Simone.'

She blenched a little, because although his formidable will had reined back the dark fury she sensed its presence not very far below the surface. Well, she was brave enough to cope. It wasn't going to be easy, but she had made her decision and she was going to stick to it. Angus was the only man she would ever be able to love like this, and she was not going to give him up without a fight to the end.

She half expected him to rush her into the bedroom but he had himself well in hand once more. In fact, as he made her coffee and chatted casually, it was only the surging rush of her hormones and the slight tenderness of her lips that kept that single, searing kiss in her mind.

'Have you really given up modelling?' he asked, pouring boiling water on to the ground coffee.

'Yes, I've given up. I'd decided to do that when I met you last year. It's an artificial world, and although I enjoyed it I only ever did it for the money.' She hesitated, then went on, 'My mother wanted me to do it, and when you're fifteen you do what your mother tells you... Well, I did, anyway. And it's been good to me.

I've made enough money to keep me for the rest of my life.'

'So what are you going to do, for the rest of your life? Retire?' He made it sound as though she'd decided to take up a career as an axe-murderer.

She grinned. 'No, I'd go mad. I'm going to do a few courses at university, just for interest, and I'm going to write.'

The smell of coffee was delicious, reminding her that she hadn't eaten any breakfast that morning. She looked around the kitchen, modernised some years ago when exposed brickwork was all the rage, and caught sight of a biscuit jar. 'May I have something to eat?'

For the first time real humour warmed his eyes. 'I should have known,' he said, and got out some crackers and cheese. 'Have you ever done any writing?'

'Oh, yes. I've had two books published. Mysteries.'

His brows lifted. This time she had got through that impervious layer of courtesy. 'Under your own name?'

'Well, under my full name. Simone Atkinson. They've done quite well, got good reviews for the most part.'

He nodded. 'I must read them.'

'Do you like mysteries?'

'I read anything,' he said calmly, pouring the coffee into two mugs. 'There, take that through there out on to the veranda. It's warm enough to sit outside and the view is magnificent.'

'What have you been doing this last year?' she asked when they were seated in comfortable old wicker chairs. Sinbad came prowling along the veranda and jumped up on to the cushion of a third one. 'Apart from feeding Sinbad; from her size, that must be a full-time job.'

Angus stretched long legs up on to the veranda rail. 'Like finder, like cat, I suppose. I've been working on the storage of electricity, and I think I'm making progress.'

'Good,' she said cheerfully.

'Why,' he asked in that level tone that somehow held a lethal hint of ruthlessness, 'did you come back?'

She shrugged. 'Because as well as the sex,' she said with all the calmness she could muster, 'we had good times together. I've never met another man whose company I enjoyed more.'

'Even though it was a lie, even though I set you up so that I could seduce you?'

There seemed no end to the humiliation this man could inflict on her, but she wasn't going to give him the satisfaction of letting him see how much he could hurt.

'Even then,' she murmured, watching the hard, forceful lines of his profile through drooping lashes. 'And I don't believe it was all a lie; you seemed to enjoy yourself just as much as I did.'

He was watching a bird dive into the sea. 'That's what I intended to do,' he said tonelessly. 'I saw your address on Julia's pad and I deliberately went up to see whether I could persuade you into an affair. I didn't expect any resistance.'

'And why not?' Her voice was just as steady as his.

His lip curled. 'Because when I bought that painting your husband told me that you were insatiable, that no one man could satisfy you. He seemed quite proud of it. I felt a kind of sick contempt for you and for him, poor devil, and when I heard he'd shot himself I wasn't surprised. Nor was I surprised when I met you in Virginia City, and it appeared you were enjoying some sort of fling with the photographer.'

'Chris,' she said, white-lipped at Jason's betrayal. 'You certainly didn't need much evidence for your—*assumptions*, did you?'

'He hinted at it and you didn't deny it. And I gathered from something Julia dropped that it was true.'

'Perhaps Julia wasn't as unbiased as she could have been. She wanted you for herself,' she retorted icily. 'She also told you that she had suggested she get another model for the shoot after my mother died, didn't she? Which was only half the truth.'

He shrugged. 'Was it?'

'It was. She asked for that day, and I gave it because I'd contracted to do the shoot.' Simone's mouth curved in a bleak smile. 'One of the reasons I got to the top was that I was completely professional. But Julia is not usually a liar. She must have wanted you badly.'

He said baldly, 'I never slept with her.'

She was glad of that, but she wasn't going to admit it. However, she wasn't going to let the fashion editor's insinuations fester, either. Deliberately she stated, 'I had no affair or relationship with Chris.'

'I realise that now. But you didn't object when Chris hinted that you did. He certainly seemed possessive of you.'

'One thing I discovered very early on,' she told him cynically, 'is that when you're in that business it doesn't pay to antagonise the photographer. He can make your life hell if he wants to. I've developed methods of dealing with them. Making them look fools is not one of them.'

'Does anything surprise you?' he demanded roughly. 'You didn't turn a hair when I admitted that I followed you up to Wainui Cove purely to get you into bed.'

Simone shrugged and drank some more coffee. 'I'd more or less worked out that you had nefarious designs on my body, but, if that was so, why did it take you a fortnight to get me there?'

His mouth etched a grim, self-contemptuous smile. 'I'm no seducer. I'd never done that before. You made me despise myself.'

She sensed that he was evading her question, but for now she let him get away with it. 'Is that why you left? Because you despised yourself?'

He put his coffee-mug on to the floor and got to his feet, taking hers and setting it beside his, then drawing her to her feet. 'One of the reasons,' he said savagely. 'I didn't know what the hell was going on. It was clear

that you had been a virgin, that your husband had lied.
I felt a total and complete heel, but I could do nothing
about it. I couldn't give you love, if that was what you
wanted.' His hands slid up her arms, warm and hard
and compelling, the hands of a man who worked hard.
'But now you say it's not,' he said softly, his eyes fixed
on the soft indentation in her upper lip, 'and so I don't
need to feel guilty any more. Come and let me show you
what it's like to make love, Simone.'

'You've already shown me.'

Angus laughed, deep and soft and mocking. 'No, the
first time is never much for a woman. This time I'll take
it slow and easy, until you want me so much that you
can't speak, you can only moan and scream with it, and
then I'll show you just how much you *can* want, you
fire-headed witch.'

Deep inside her some romantic, fragile part cried, Not
like this, not in lust and hunger, but, in spite of his determination not to admit to any softer feelings than lust,
there was tenderness in his eyes, in his mouth and the
touch of his hands. And she had come too far to back
out now.

Her mouth trembled into a smile. 'OK,' she said, and
kissed him gently.

Afterwards she never knew whether he had carried
her in through the open french windows to the bedroom,
but she remembered the exquisite care with which he'd
undressed her, the shaking hands and the leap of fire in
his iron-cast face, and the gentleness with which he'd
touched the slender perfection of her body.

And the swift upwelling of desire, the sensuous, incandescent pleasures of skin against skin, light against
dark, of blazing hair sifting through lean, dark fingers,
of ivory skin against bronze, of feminine sleekness
against male hardness, of the smooth swell of muscles
against the soft fullness of breast, the fierce male thrust
into the feminine encirclement, being taken over, trans-
lated from the ordinary to some place beyond the world

where this was the ultimate, this slow accumulation of sensation into an ecstasy that rocked them both over an edge and into oblivion.

The first thing Simone noticed was her breathing, fast and harsh, and the thud of her heart in her throat, in her temples, in every pulse-point through her body. Intermingled with them were the deep, dragging breaths Angus was taking, the wild thunder of his heart easing slowly, so slowly, into something like normality.

Then the delicious sensation of surrender, the consciousness of lying flat on the big bed, legs outstretched, arms caught around the smooth tension of his back, revelling in his weight, his heat, the golden aftermath of passion, as wonderful in its own way as the rapture that led to it. Deep inside her the after-shocks were still shuddering round him.

He had moved slightly so that she could breathe, turning his face on the fiery veil of her hair across the pillow. She opened her eyes a fraction, dazzled by the sun through the window, the sound of the waves on the beach, the loud purring of the cat that leapt gracefully up on to the bed and with the unconquerable imperturbability of its kind arranged itself beside her feet.

Simone shook with the effort to stop a giggle.

Angus froze. 'What's the matter?'

'Nothing,' she said, allowing the laughter free rein. 'Only that Sinbad seems to approve of this.'

He lifted himself up on one elbow and looked down the bed. Amusement softened the brilliant blue of his gaze. 'Hmm,' he said, and rolled over on to his back, linking his hands behind his head as he stared up at the ceiling.

Simone shivered, and without looking at her he flipped the quilt over her. 'This alters nothing,' he said.

She had hoped, of course, but she was prepared for this reaction. He would not be the man she loved if he had been easy to convince. Stubborn tenacity was an essential part of his character, it had got him to where he was now, and naturally it applied to all aspects of his life. He was determined not to allow himself to be caught again in the love trap, and he had the will-power to fight to the death against it. Once bitten, twice shy.

But she was stubborn too. She could fight for what she wanted, and she was not going to let go her chances of happiness just because he was intransigent, because he had been too badly hurt by a careless woman to trust his own reactions again. His opinion of Simone had to be affected by Jason's lies; she would, she vowed, change that opinion and, when she had, perhaps she would be able to tell him about that marriage. Perhaps it was a bad sign that he hadn't asked what had happened, but she was not going to give up.

'I know,' she said calmly.

He turned his head. 'Are you a masochist?'

She laughed, lifting up on her elbow to kiss the muscles of his chest. Her tongue traced a delicate line through the springy hair, and she felt his instant response with a small, secret smile.

'No, there's nothing masochistic about enjoying you,' she said sweetly, taunting him a little. 'Masochism might come into it if I did this——' she found a tight, hard little nub and licked it delicately, listening to his involuntarily indrawn breath with pleasure and a rising excitement '—and this——' tracing with her tongue a line down the rigid slab of his midriff until she came to the slight indentation of his navel '—and did nothing about it.'

She felt the tension rising like smoke from him, the coiled purpose of muscle and sinew, but she explored that interesting little depression with tentative, delicate touches of her tongue, flicking her head so that the perfumed flood of her hair curled like a silken swath across his loins.

Calloused hands clenched on her shoulders, dragging her up to lie across his rapidly hardening body. 'Witch,' he said deeply, flames glittering in his gaze as he took in the softly blossoming line of her mouth, the sensual laughter teasing him in her expression. 'Are you insatiable, Simone? Do you want more, or does it amuse you to torment me?'

She shook her head, something in the uneven note of his voice warning her. 'Why should I torment you?' she said, looking her love, because she couldn't yet speak it. Had his wife done this, teased him until he surrendered and then refused him?

'Women can be cruel,' he said, but the words came without much expression as Simone touched him lovingly, her slumbrous eyes revealing far more than she had said, the smile that curved her lips becoming fixed.

He laughed, but he pulled her down on to him, taking her with something like desperation, until the need and the power turned once more to a raging fulfilment, and she lay sweat-soaked and exhausted, drifting off to sleep with her cheek pillowed on his chest, the mingled thunder of their pulses serving as a lullaby.

An hour later she awoke alone in the bed, Sinbad's purrs blending with the sound of the waves and the clear, bell tones of a tui from the enormous flame tree out in the garden.

There was no other sound. Yawning, aching pleasurably, Simone got up and draped the quilt around her, thereby putting an end to Sinbad's sleep, and found her way to a small, spartan bathroom. It had a shower, but she ran a bath, stretching her limbs with a sinuous, sensual pleasure as she climbed into the soft, silky water.

She washed the sweat of their lovemaking from her skin and her hair, and lay back for long, languorous moments with a sultry little smile on her lips, before climbing out.

'Well, Sinbad,' she said to the cat, who slitted her eyes and stretched her claws before turning over on the bathmat, 'so far, so good. Now I just have to make myself as necessary to him as his breath and his blood.

And that is not going to be easy, because we have a tough, obstinate man to deal with.'

She needed to feel that she had an ally in this undertaking, the most important of her life. As there was no other applicant Sinbad was elected for the position.

Wrapped once more in the quilt, she went back into the bedroom, dressed, borrowed his hairbrush to restore her locks to some sort of order, and washed the brush free of the clinging red strands before making the bed. There was still no sound from the rest of the house, and when she went out on to the veranda she realised why. On one of the headlands that enclosed the bay she could see Angus; he was standing, staring out across the estuary.

'He looks lonely,' she said to the cat. 'Proud, and arrogant, even a little bit cruel, but so lonely. Well, he won't ever have to be lonely again. I wonder how we're going to be able to convince him of it?'

She had made lunch when he returned, setting the small table in the big farmhouse kitchen with a cloth and silver, cooking a Spanish omelette before putting the kettle on. A tiny tremor of—fear?—shook her stomach, but she hoped there was no sign of it when he came in. Eyes unshadowed, she smiled at him, although her heart sank at the grimness of his expression.

'It's just about ready,' she said cheerfully.

His expression didn't alter. 'If I needed a housekeeper I can afford to employ one,' he replied.

But he watched her too closely. Simone lifted her brows. 'Of course,' she said coolly. 'Did I give you the impression that you were going to be able to use me as a housekeeper? Sorry. I have no intention of turning into a household slave.'

'Then what's this all about?'

Her eyes gleamed with laughter. 'I'm hungry,' she said simply, inviting him to share the joke.

Reluctantly he smiled. 'When have you ever not been?' But even as she dished up the meal he said quietly, 'I meant what I said, Simone. I don't need a woman except for one basic reason.'

'That's OK,' she said, ignoring the pain that clawed at her. 'I don't *need* a man, either.'

'Then why——?'

'Why did I come?' She slid her own omelette, not much smaller than his, on to a plate and joined him at the table. 'I told you.'

'You want me.'

She nodded. 'Eat up. It's good.'

'But you must have wanted other men,' he persisted calmly, not moving, 'and you haven't moved in with them. You were a virgin that last time, and you haven't slept with anyone since we made love.'

'How do you know?'

His wide shoulders moved in a shrug. Eyeing her composed face as she made hearty inroads into her omelette, he said angrily, 'I know. So why are you here, Simone?'

'I'm twenty-six,' she said collectedly. 'You are the only man who has ever made me feel like this. If I did the sensible thing and turned my back on you, left you to the solitude you so clearly prefer, I might never get you out of my system. I refuse to spend the rest of my life wondering whether I could have done it if I'd tried. So I'm going to try.' Her mouth stretched in the painful semblance of a smile. 'Jason—my husband—told me that familiarity and satisfied desire destroyed the hunger and the passion. He channelled all his sexuality into his painting so that there was nothing left for real life. Look at it this way; if he was right, then we both stand to gain—we can sate ourselves and get it out of our systems. But it has to be more than an affair. An affair can be exciting, romantic. I think it needs mundane domesticity to induce boredom. I'll try not to get in your way, and you'll have to keep out of mine. I have a deadline to fulfil.'

It was impossible to tell what Angus was thinking. His face was the same dark mask, harshly delineated by the sunlight through the window that she had seen on the street in Virginia City. Then, as though the lies she had told satisfied him, he picked up knife and fork and began to eat. After a moment she too resumed her meal, although all her appetite had fled.

'So you want to move in with me?' he asked indifferently.

Hastily veiling her eyes with her lashes so that he couldn't see the mingled pain and relief, she said in an equally neutral voice, 'It seems to be the most likely way to get so accustomed to each other that tedium will begin to set in.'

He ate another mouthful. 'Very well.' The deep voice was cool and crisp, without emotion.

Simone fought down a great leap of satisfaction. 'I'll pay half the expenses, of course,' she said in a businesslike voice.

His brow lifted ironically. 'All right.'

She nodded. 'I'll go back to Auckland and make the arrangements.'

'I see you have it all worked out.' He waited until she had eaten everything on her plate before saying casually, 'Just one thing, though. Have I your word that you'll be available to me whenever I want you, not get in my way, and go whenever I tell you?'

He spelled it out with as much casual cruelty as he could; perhaps even then he wanted her to go.

Simone looked at him with her mouth tilted in a strange, unamused little smile, her slanting eyes shadowed, enigmatic, filled with secrets. 'Yes,' she said simply. 'No tears, no pleas, no regrets, and no bones broken. Isn't that the way it goes?'

He gave no quarter. 'Yes.'

She nodded and held out her hand. After a moment he took it; ignoring the sizzle of awareness that powered along her nerves, she said, 'Let's shake on it.'

CHAPTER NINE

SIMONE left Angus without a backwards glance, but her heart stayed behind, as securely his as though he held it in one of those lean, dark hands that could be so fiercely possessive yet so gentle.

She reached the hotel around six, and instead of eating dinner found to her shock and surprise that she had no appetite. So she sat down with a sheet of paper and began to make a list.

First of all, she had to buy a car. Angus had spelled out with hard inflexibility just what she could expect from him—exactly nothing except his superb love-making, and, although Simone had every intention of changing his mind, she was not going to become dependent on him. Whatever his ex-wife had been like, whatever the reasons she had had for marrying Angus, he had to understand that they were not going to be repeated in this relationship.

After a restless night she bought her new car, a sleek German model admired as much for its sturdiness as for its glamour, and when the formalities were done drove it back to the hotel and checked out. Her entire worldly goods were in two large suitcases, plus a packing case that was on its way from New York to Auckland via ship. It didn't seem much, she thought ironically, for over ten years of living, but she had not wanted to bring with her the clutter of that other life.

Also in the back of the car was a computer, with hard disc and printer, brand new, as well as all the necessary paper and files, stationery and reference books.

Driving carefully, she arrived as the sun went down behind the hills in the centre of the island.

Accompanied by Sinbad, Angus came out to the car, and looked his surprise as his gaze fell on the packing cases in the back seat.

'I had some buying to do,' she explained.

'I can see that,' he said, his voice non-committal.

She smiled. 'Yes.' Did he resent the fact that she had her own money? Well, he would have to learn to cope with it.

'I expected you back earlier,' he said, not as though it mattered.

Simone wondered whether he had watched the track for her arrival, hoping that she would be early as much as she had longed to get there all through the long, busy day. 'I had a lot to do. Want to help me carry the stuff in?'

'I'll do it. You go and do whatever you need to do to freshen up.'

She hesitated, then yielded to impulse and the deep, aching need that had underlain all of her actions since she had seen him that first time, half a world away. Reaching up, she kissed him lightly. He was very still, but he didn't pull away, although his tension communicated itself to her by a variety of subtle ways, all open and obvious to the senses of love.

'OK,' she said softly.

His arms contracted around her, bruising, but after only a second he put her away from him. 'Hurry up, before it gets dark,' was all he said, but there was a tell-tale unevenness in his voice that set her heart to singing.

Something that smelled delicious simmered in the oven. The table was set—with one place.

Did he trust her so little? Her heart contracted into a tight, hard knot, but she angled her chin as she went past the door into the bathroom. Sooner or later he'd learn that unless he threw her out she would always be there for him—and even if he did throw her out he was going to have to work damned hard to make her believe that he no longer wanted her. She loved him so much that she was prepared to give him as long as he needed to learn that he felt more for her than casual desire, however irresistible that was.

When she emerged from the bathroom he had transferred her suitcase into the big bedroom where they had made love the day before, while the boxes containing the computer, disc-drive and printer were waiting in the room next to it, a small, unused room with a bookshelf in the corner.

'We'll look at them later,' she said cheerfully, loving him with her eyes as he looked up from the manual. 'Is dinner ready?'

His smile just escaped being a taunt. 'You're starving, right?'

'I see you're beginning to know me,' she said solemnly. 'I wasn't known as "The Mouth" just for these gorgeous, pouting lips, you know.'

His glance sharpened, intensified. She felt a tingling in those lips, and had to fight to hold the smile. Whatever she had to do in these next few weeks, the one thing he mustn't learn too soon was that she loved him. He had the sort of abrasive principles that would send her away. Because he was convinced he couldn't love her, he would believe that accepting her love would be unfair.

'When I first started modelling,' she said, pretending not to notice the darkness of desire in his expression, 'I was just fifteen, and I was still growing. I ate everything in sight. The nickname was inevitable.'

'What were you doing modelling at fifteen?'

She shrugged, preceding him down the hall to the kitchen. 'My mother sent my photograph to a modelling competition, which I won. Part of the prize was an interview with the proprietor of a modelling agency in New York, and she offered me a chance to go there.'

'And your mother let you go?'

She said flatly, 'She came with me.'

'I see.' He seated her then went across to the bench. 'You had no father by then, I gather.'

'Yes, I had a father.' It still hurt, after all these years. She went on steadily, 'My mother left him. He died about a year later, before I saw him again. He was a diabetic, and I don't think he looked after himself properly when we left.'

Angus tipped stew into a serving dish, vegetables into another, his movements quick and deft. 'What was he like?'

'Big,' she said softly. 'Handsome, too. He was a motor mechanic, a quiet, easygoing man. My mother said he had no ambition, but he was happy doing a job he loved. He was a good father.'

The serving dishes arrived on the table. Angus sat down and said, 'Help yourself. Your mother was ambitious, I take it?'

'Yes.' Simone lifted the lid from the dish, her nostrils wrinkling appreciatively at the savoury smell. 'This looks delicious. Can I get you some?'

He handed his plate over and she ladled a large helping. As she passed it back he asked quietly, 'Was she as beautiful as you?'

'More so. But she had never had the opportunity to exploit her looks, as she used to remind me frequently when I got bored with the whole business.'

'So she used you to satisfy her own frustrated ambition, so that she could live the life she wanted vicariously.'

'Yes,' she admitted. 'It happens, Angus. And she wasn't a wicked mother; she was good to me in her own way.'

'But not so good to your father.'

'No. He loved me for what I was, not because I was the latest "look", not because I earned a vast amount of money.'

Angus's thoughts were shielded by his incredible lashes. Simone studied the shadows of them on his lean, dark cheeks, the grim set to his mouth. 'But that was them,' she said deliberately, 'and this is us, Angus.'

He lifted his lids. 'Is the past so easy to shuck off?'

'I don't know,' she said, bracing herself at the hard anger that gleamed in his glance. 'Is it?'

Shoulders lifting in a massive shrug, he drawled, 'Forget about it.' His narrowed gaze surveyed the pure lines of her face, the slender length of her throat and the soft promise of her breasts beneath the warm wool shirt. He smiled, and her pulse began to increase.

That was all it took. Just one smile. Oh, she was fathoms deep in love with this hard, enigmatic man who was still bound to the past, bound by silken, invisible ties to a woman who had hurt him so deeply that he had vowed never to be vulnerable again. Well, vulnerability didn't necessarily mean weakness. She had discovered that; in time, and with the help of her love, he would too.

If she could stick it out for long enough.

'There's an old desk in one of the other rooms; it might be adequate for you, but you'll need to buy a decent one, as well as an ergonomically correct chair.'

She jerked free of the miasma of pain. 'Yes, I will. Buy one, I mean. I don't want sore shoulders or repetitive strain injury. Is this house yours, or are you renting it?'

'I bought it with the idea of building a new one, but I've done nothing about it yet.'

Over dinner they discussed the sort of house he might like to build, and then he helped her set up the computer. After that they went to bed and made love, but this time it was different, this time he wasn't going to let shock and desire overcome him. He took it slowly, using his immense experience to wring the last ounce of response from her until she was moaning with need, begging him to take her, and even then he made her wait, punishing her, she thought afterwards, for her arrival in his life.

But when she cried out and reached that distant, unknowable peak of ecstasy, he held her in his arms as though he would shelter her from everything the world could throw at her, and without waiting pushed her up the slope again, until he too went under, cast away on the dark seas of desire.

She was alone again when she woke to a rich spring morning, but when she went out on to the veranda he was just coming up from the beach, Sinbad at his heels. He smiled at her with a gleam of pure, masculine possessiveness in his brilliant eyes, but no softness, none of the tenderness he showed when they made love.

Patience, she warned herself. It's worth waiting for.

After breakfast he disappeared to a room he called 'the office', where, she supposed, he invented things.

Surprisingly enough, she worked well, losing herself in the manuscript until lunchtime, when they ate and talked. Then they both worked until five, and after that there was more conversation, more discussion, the slow, fumbling process of learning to understand another human being.

And then it was time for bed, and they made white-hot love, ferocious, incandescent, and slept dreamlessly until morning.

It was a satisfying life, and, over the next weeks of changeable spring weather, Simone dared to allow herself to hope that he was beginning to appreciate her, that their lovemaking, so intense, so earthily shining and wondrous, was forging bonds as strong as her love.

One morning, just before lunch, she leaned back in her chair and stretched, when, to her astonishment—for until then they'd had no visitors—she heard a car drive up. A minute or so later there was a knock on the door.

Biting her lip, for it was stupid to feel self-conscious, she went out.

Standing outside was a woman an inch or so shorter than Simone, with hair almost exactly the same colour. She had her back to the door, and when Simone said blankly, 'Yes?' she gave a gasp and swung around, her great green eyes widening as she saw Simone.

After a moment she seemed to pull herself together. 'My name is Susan Blake,' she said quietly. 'I'd like to see Angus if I may, please.'

Jealousy, so intense that it almost ripped her heart in two, clawed through Simone, but although she could feel the colour leaching away from her skin she said in a level voice, 'I'll see what he says.'

He looked up, frowning, as she came in through the door, but the frown vanished instantly, and he said sharply, 'What's happened?'

In a voice that had lost all expression she said, 'Your ex-wife is here, and she wants to talk to you.'

The pencil he had been holding snapped clear in two pieces. His eyes went opaque and a white line appeared around his mouth. After a moment he got up. 'Does she indeed? The bitch,' he said softly. 'You can tell her that I've no interest in seeing her at all.'

Simone shook her head. 'Tell her yourself,' she said, realising how hopeless everything was. He was still bound to the woman, still locked into some kind of combat with her memory. Nothing Simone had done, nothing she could do, not her love, or the last two happy weeks, would ever be enough to prise him free of this incubus of unresolved emotions.

He got up, looming over her like a colossus, implacable, looking at her with blind eyes. 'I'm not going anywhere near her, the slut,' he asserted in a voice that had no emotion in it at all.

'Then she obviously has to come to you.' The voice from the door was ironic, perfectly controlled. 'Hello, Angus.'

He swung around to stare at the slender, beautifully groomed woman, his expression so rigidly controlled that the effort it needed was clear. 'Susan,' he said in that soft, terrifying voice.

Simone turned away but his hand caught her, held her in a grip that bruised. 'No,' he said indifferently, 'you can stay, I've nothing to hide from you.'

His ex-wife stood very still, her green eyes fixed on his face. Something about that stillness revealed real fear.

Simone felt a vast, inconvenient sympathy. 'What do you want?' she asked her huskily. 'I'll go if what you have to say to Angus is private.'

The green eyes widened, then fell to the hand that shackled Simone's wrist. 'It's all right,' the older woman said hurriedly. 'I just came to tell Angus that—that I'm getting married again.'

'Why bother?' Angus's voice was smooth and emotionless. 'You didn't bother to tell me you were leaving.'

Susan winced, her eyes darting from his face to Simone's. She licked her lips. 'I don't want us to be enemies for the rest of our lives. And I wanted to tell you that I was sorry.'

His forefinger moved up and down the inside of Simone's wrist, stroking across the vulnerable veins, the fragile bones. 'For what?'

'For marrying you when I didn't love you. And for leaving you the way I did. It was a lousy thing to do, and I've regretted it ever since.'

'OK,' he said indifferently. 'I deserved it, because I didn't love you when I married you either.'

'I know.' Susan looked again at the woman beside him. 'I'm glad you've finally come to see it. I don't want your blessing or anything like that, but the man I'm going to marry said that I needed to apologise for behaving like a bitch.' Her eyes flicked to Angus's unmoving, implacable face, then back to Simone's shuttered expression. She drew a ragged breath. 'I'm glad you've found someone else,' she finished hastily. 'Perhaps she'll be able to give you what I never could.'

That was the bitterest irony of all. For Simone realised that all that she had done, the compromises she had made, the love she had given so freely, had all been wasted. Angus didn't love her—never would. She had only to see him with this woman who had thrown away his love to realise that.

His finger was still smoothing over the vulnerable skin. 'I'll see you out,' he offered, still in that same unemotional voice.

Susan shook her head. 'It doesn't matter.'

'Is this—the man you're engaged to—out in the car?'

'No, he made me come up by myself.' She dampened her lips again, glancing from one to the other, her expression almost bewildered, as though she couldn't understand what was going on. 'I hope you'll be happy,' she said, and left, her heels tap-tapping on the floor, her back held straight with the most rigid control.

Angus let Simone's hand go. He said nothing, merely turned away, the primal male grace for once not noticeable. Had Susan's confession that she was marrying again hurt so much?

Simone watched, but she didn't follow him as he went out. She sat down limply in the nearest chair, listening to the engine as the car outside went up the hill towards the road, wondering if Angus was hearing the knell of all his dreams in the mundane sound.

So she had gambled, and lost. He still loved the woman who had betrayed him. And where, she thought, trying to overcome the aching void in her heart, where exactly did that leave her?

Wearily, her bones aching, she got up and walked out on to the veranda, unseeing eyes scanning the sunlit waters with complete indifference. Nothing stirred inside the house as she fought perhaps the hardest battle of her life, torn between an unbearable sense of betrayal and the reckless courage that had set her on the path to this disillusion.

She had been so sure that he was learning to love her; they had so much in common, as well as the blazing rapture that was ever-fresh, ever-newborn each time they came together in passion. But it had all been for nothing. She was desirable to him because she looked like Susan,

hat was all. She was a pale substitute for the woman
ie had never stopped loving.

Her first instinct was to go, to leave him with his
memories and his insulting, reluctant desire, but Simone
was made of sterner stuff than that. As she watched the
sunlight dancing across the estuary she decided that she
had another chance. Susan was getting married again,
putting a period to any lingering, subconscious hopes
ie might have had. Surely that meant he would have to
face the fact, once and for all, that it was over. Perhaps
ie would realise that he could make a satisfactory new
ife with Simone.

Could she live happily with him, knowing that he loved
the other woman?

She climbed up on to the veranda rail and stretched
her legs along it, her head turned so that she could see
this view that she had learnt to love, to rely on for peace
and the ease of her soul. Sinbad leapt gracefully up and
arranged herself on Simone's lap, purring.

Was she courageous enough to live with him, offering
love and receiving affection and passion, knowing that
when he looked at her he saw another woman?

Oh, yes, she could do that. In time Susan's face would
be replaced by hers. But would her face in time be replaced by another's, belonging to some other tall woman
with hair a true, glowing red? Was Angus just hooked
on the physical attributes, as Jason had been?

A sudden chill dimmed the sun. No, she thought, for
Jason her body had been an unhealthy obsession. He
had used her in the most insulting way of all, used the
passion she aroused to feed his muse. Angus enjoyed her
with robust, lusty sensuality, making sure that she was
taken to the heights of rapture.

And in spite of his warnings when she had returned
to him, he did not see her as a mere body. These last
weeks together had reinforced her conviction that she
and he were compatible in many more ways than the
purely physical. Their minds struck sparks from each

other. They shared the same basic viewpoints, the same sense of honour; each discussion, even their arguments, were a delight. They even shared a sense of humour. Which was more than he had shared with Susan, who did not, she thought cattily, look as though she had any sense of humour at all.

He made no noise when he came out through the french windows, but Simone sensed his presence, turning her head to look at him. Not that there was anything to read; his face was impassive, all signs of emotion suppressed.

'I need to go away,' he announced flatly.

She nodded, afraid to speak in case her voice gave too much away.

'I'm sorry,' he said after a moment.

She strove to see through the shuttered blue eyes to the man beneath, but his armour was too good.

'OK,' she said huskily.

And that was that. He left in the Range Rover with a few clothes, and the sole thing Simone had to console herself was that he clearly expected her to stay, even if it was just to look after Sinbad.

During the next endless, lonely days she was racked with conflicting decisions, able to concentrate only on writing. Should she go? Was it hopeless to keep on with this, hoping that he would learn to love her when he had spent the past six years in thrall to another woman? Angus was a very controlled man, but behind the control there was an intensity she had been wary of right from the first. Could he put away his old love and learn to love again, or was he bound forever to Susan, whatever she did, however many years passed?

Simone was sitting in the lounger on the veranda, with the rising sun picking out the weariness in her face, when he came back, walking silently, lithely across the wet grass. Warily, her expression still and set, she watched him, her long fingers sifting through Sinbad's fur, unable to speak.

He looked—tired, she thought, her eyes scanning the hard-honed angles of his face; yet there was something in his expression she had never seen before. Peace?

'You look like Hine, the dawn maiden,' he said as he came up the steps. 'Pale and beautiful with the sun tangled in your hair.'

She said nothing, hope and fear choking in her throat.

'Can you ever forgive me?' he asked quietly, the deep blue eyes, eyes the colour of a summer twilight, never leaving her face.

'What for?'

He smiled sardonically. 'For treating you like a mistress instead of the love of my life.'

She stared at him, unable to accept that he meant what he said. His mouth twisted; he sat down beside her on the lounger and took her hand, holding it in his long, warm one as he said, 'I was sure I'd never stop loving Susan, you know, even when she left me and I thought I hated her. And then I met you, and the attraction was just as instantaneous, just as potent. I was appalled, vowing never to give in to it again, never to leave myself open for the hell I went through when she went. Possibly you don't know, but she left me for Morgan Caird.'

Simone drew in a sharp, horrified breath.

'Yes.' Angus lifted her hand and kissed the wrist, his lips lingering against the fragile blue veins. 'He didn't know Susan was married, but he met Clary—my sister—when he was still living with her. As you can imagine, it caused a lot of pain before we managed to straighten it out. When I saw that he really did love Clary, that she loved him, I was able to accept their marriage, but having him so closely related kept the wound open and raw.'

'I knew there was something about him,' she said at last, her voice husky. 'You went—away, when his name came up.'

'Yes; you're quick and astute. I like Morgan, I admire him, I trust him, but at bottom I saw him as the man who stole my wife.'

'I can understand that,' she said painfully. 'You must have loved her very much.'

He gave a cynical smile. 'I didn't love her at all,' he revealed calmly. 'I wanted her, I was very possessive of her, but it had to be on my terms. She married me when she was at her lowest ebb; she'd had a relationship with a married man, and she was shattered when he went back to his wife. She was being propositioned by someone in the industry, someone with the power to keep her out of work, and I think she was exhausted, mentally and emotionally. She also had no money; she has never been good with finances—everything she earned, and for a while she was earning good money, just slid through her fingers. When I came along she saw a refuge.'

Simone said cautiously, 'She recognised that rock-bottom integrity. It appeals to women. She knew she'd be safe with you.'

'Perhaps. She told me she loved me; I wasn't so besotted that I was unable to see the truth, but I was sure that in time she'd learn to love me. But she didn't. And I wasn't able to—I'm afraid I turned nasty. I frightened her so much she ran away. Hell, sometimes I frighten myself. I was jealous, I behaved like an animal when she left me——'

'I think you're being hard on yourself.' Simone tried to speak objectively. 'You loved her; naturally you were desolated when she left.'

'I've been nursing my wounded pride and thoughts of revenge for six years,' he corrected harshly. 'I'm not a compassionate man, Simone, I'm a vengeful one. If I'd been more aware I'd have realised that love is not selfish. I would have wanted her to be happy. I was able to overcome my anger and resentment and bitterness when I realised that the only way Clary could be happy was with Morgan. And I knew, well before Susan left me, that she was not happy. It was possessiveness that made me insist she stay with me, and greed, and selfishness—not love, or anything like it.'

'How do you know?'

He touched her cheek. 'When she turned up here the other day I looked at her, and it was like looking at an old schoolteacher. I felt nothing. And then I realised that I had wasted all the time you and I have had together because I refused to admit my need, my hunger for revenge. You had taken over my cold heart completely, fired it to life, given me so much... I had to go away so that I could work out what I felt, what I was going to do.'

'And what are you going to do?' she asked gravely.

'I'm going to ask you to marry me, as I should have done last year in Northland. And if you say no, as you have every right to do, I'm not going to stop wooing you until I have convinced you that it was Susan who came along at the wrong time; she was the pale echo, the forerunner, you the real thing. If I'd met you first I would never have looked at her. I knew that, I think, when I bought the painting. It was you I wanted, not Susan; it was the woman I saw shimmering with repressed sensuality——'

'I hated those paintings,' Simone said, shuddering. 'I made Jason's agent burn them all, except that one, and I didn't even know it existed.'

'Are you going to make me burn this one?'

She looked up at him. 'Would you?'

'Yes,' he said simply. 'But I hope you won't. Whatever happened in your marriage—and I hope one day you'll be able to tell me—Jason Sinclair painted it with love as well as frustrated passion.'

She bit her lip. 'I know,' she admitted, at last able to understand something of the torment Jason had endured. 'And I failed him.'

'He failed himself.'

She hesitated, then said with a miraculous lightening of the burden she had been shouldering ever since her marriage, 'All right, then. We'll keep it.'

'Does that mean you're going to marry me?'

'What will happen if I say yes?'

He smiled, his eyes brilliant, revealed to her as they had never been before. His dark countenance would never be soft, but she looked up and saw love there, an open avowal that set her heart singing.

'The same that will happen if you say no. I'll tell you that I love you for being the determined, courageous, laughing woman that you are, and we'll get married and live long and happily, producing books and babies——'

'And inventions,' she finished triumphantly, allowing him to draw her to her feet, much to Sinbad's irritation.

Angus laughed deep in his throat, the clear, jubilant laughter of a triumphant lover, and held her for a moment, his hands tender around her face, his eyes gleaming with satisfaction and joy—a deep, heartfelt warmth that overset all her remaining defences.

'Yes. All of those. Simone, I love you more than I can tell you. I must have fallen head over heels that first night, when I watched you eat your way delicately through the enormous meal, and laugh and joke with the others, while you kept darting little, suspicious looks at me as though I was the ghost at the feast. I wanted so much to be the one you joked with...'

'I was afraid,' she confessed for the first time. 'I knew I had never met anyone like you before, and I was afraid that you were like so many men—that you wanted with your eyes and your hormones.'

'Tell me about your husband.'

Angus understood her better sometimes than she did erself. She sighed, but her eyes met his, true and honest. Jason was—impotent.'

Comprehension and shock appeared in his face, in his voice. 'Poor devil.'

'Yes. I've come to realise that in his own way he loved me, but he wouldn't ask for help. He was embarrassed— o, humiliated—by what he saw as a fatal flaw, but he onvinced himself that as long as he didn't touch me he ould continue to paint me. In some ways he was the xact opposite of all the men who were greedy, who saw me as a thing to be possessed, not as a person.'

'Did you think I was like that?'

'I hoped you weren't. You seemed more attracted to ulia, which was hopeful, although that hurt too.'

He kissed her gently. 'That night in Virginia City I ad a drink with her, then I left. When she got back to uckland she contacted me, and I took her out several imes. She must have guessed that I wanted you because he skilfully fed me a few half-truths; that was how I iscovered that your mother had died that night. And hat you were up at Wainui Cove, although she didn't ell me that. I saw the note on her desk when I came to ollect her from work one day. But she wanted more han I could give her, and I knew I never could feel like hat for her, so I let her down as gently as I could.'

'And came up to Wainui Cove to seduce me.'

He made a grimace. 'That's what I told myself I was oing to do. But somehow things didn't ring true. I xpected a greedy little sensualist, and you just weren't ke that. You were quick, and intelligent, and funny, nd you were prepared to risk your life to save a kitten. After that accident, when I realised that I could have ost you, I felt sick. I realised that I wanted much more han an affair with you.'

He touched her lips, the high swoop of her cheekbone, vith fingers that trembled. 'And, although I didn't get damned wink of sleep that night when we slept together, somehow seduction was the last thing on my mind. I decided to wait, to get to know you. Then I went to that damned party, and the first thing I saw when I walked into that bloody room was you smouldering up at Fleming. I'd heard the rumours, of course, and I'd seen you together a year before at a consulate dinner in San Francisco. You seemed besotted with him; I watched you with murder in my heart. When I saw you with him again all I could think of was that you'd been amusing yourself with me.'

'So that's where I saw you,' she breathed. 'I remember now; you stood in the shadows and I felt you watching me.'

'Yes.' His mouth tightened, then relaxed. 'Your eyes went straight through me,' he said deliberately.

'Caine and I are friends,' she explained, holding his gaze with hers, determined to make him understand. 'I like him very much, but there's never been any sort of relationship between us. The night of the De Roque party I was furious because I'd been manoeuvred into wearing that damned dress, so I flirted with him. It was stupid and I was sorry afterwards because I thought someone might gossip at Petra, but I knew Caine wouldn't get the wrong idea.'

He nodded, but said grimly, 'I thought it was happening all over again—that I was a fool, lost in a wasteland of bitter passion, unable to control it, or myself, and a lesser man because of it.'

Simone made a soft noise and Angus smiled crookedly. 'I went back to Wainui Cove determined to have you; I told myself that if you were so free with your favours why shouldn't I enjoy you as much as the other men you'd slept with? So we made love, and it was the most wonderful thing that ever happened to me. But you were a virgin. I got suspicious all over again.'

'And you accused me of refusing to sleep with my husband.'

'It was like Susan all over again,' he said quietly. 'I felt that she had *refused* to love me, that she wanted to flirt and laugh and tease, but not to love. I hated myself for the way I behaved to her, the unbearable, uncontrollable anger and jealousy I felt. I blamed her for making an animal of me. That's why I left—so that you couldn't do that to me again.'

'And now?'

He bent to touch his mouth to her forehead. 'I discovered that it was me who did it to me—not Susan, not you. I love you, Simone. I want to devote the rest of my life to making you happy.' He drew a deep, harsh breath, holding her gently, as though she was something unmanageably precious to him.

She bit her lip. 'I don't deliberately flirt, Angus—well, only occasionally. The woman in the photographs is not me. Sometimes I've looked at them and wondered how an ordinary, sensible person like me can look so—so decadent.'

He laughed, tilting her face so that he could see into her eyes, his own clear, like crystals of darkest sapphire, transparent and beautiful so that she could see his thoughts, the love she had longed for, reflected there.

'You look like every man's temptress because that's what you are,' he said softly, kissing her eyes closed. 'But they, poor devils, have to imagine, while I know how sane and whole and satisfying you are, my own heart, my dearest love, my perfect one. That *decadence* is sweet sensuality, and I know that you are nothing like poor Susan; you don't need me to keep you, or to lean on, or to get you out of a sticky situation.'

Simone thought her breath was permanently lodged in her throat. She kissed his chin, and said, smiling mistily through tears that wouldn't go away, 'Even though you had to minister to me twice—once after we rescued Sinbad, and then after that accident?'

'You'd have managed,' he said, kissing her eyelashes. 'Just as you managed to move in here. God help me, I think you could probably manage to get to the moon if you decided to! You came here and gave me everything, cunning as Circe, and while I took what you gave me I fell in love with you more and more. Even before Susan came I was beginning to realise that you were the woman I should have waited for, the love that was real and genuine.'

Simone murmured something and turned her face into his throat, breathing in the evocative masculine scent of him, with her heart swelling so lightly, so rapturously, that she thought it might fly from her chest.

'I know now, you see, that you love me,' he whispered. 'That makes all the difference.'

She nodded, and they stood there for long moments, locked in each other's arms, savouring the sense of haven, of coming home at last. Perched on the veranda rail, Sinbad watched them, both blue eye and gold wise and smugly satisfied.

PRESENTS® *plus*

Meet Griff Morgan, a man on the rebound, and Sarah
Williams, a woman who *already* has a broken heart.

And then there's Sam Hardy, who simply loves 'em and leaves
'em, and Lauren Bell, who's still haunted by *one* man from
her past.

These are just some of the passionate men and women you'll
discover each month in Harlequin Presents Plus—two longer
and dramatic new romances by some of the best-loved authors
writing for Harlequin Presents. Share their exciting stories—
their heartaches and triumphs—as each falls in love.

Don't miss
THE JILTED BRIDEGROOM by Carole Mortimer
Harlequin Presents Plus #1559
and
SLEEPING PARTNERS by Charlotte Lamb
Harlequin Presents Plus #1560

Harlequin Presents Plus

The best has just gotten better!
Available in June wherever Harlequin books are sold.

HARLEQUIN SUPERROMANCE®

HARLEQUIN SUPERROMANCE NOVELS WANTS TO INTRODUCE YOU TO A DARING NEW CONCEPT IN ROMANCE...

WOMEN WHO DARE!
Bright, bold, beautiful...
Brave and caring, strong and passionate...
They're women who know their own minds
and will dare anything...
for love!

One title per month in 1993, written by popular Superromance authors, will highlight our special heroines as they face unusual, challenging and sometimes dangerous situations.

Love blooms next month with:
#553 LATE BLOOMER by Peg Sutherland
Available in June wherever Harlequin Superromance novels are sold

**Relive the romance...
Harlequin and Silhouette
are proud to present**

A program of collections of three complete novels by the most requested authors with the most requested themes. Be sure to look for one volume each month with three complete novels by top name authors.

In June: **NINE MONTHS** Penny Jordan
Stella Cameron
Janice Kaiser

Three women pregnant and alone. But a lot can happen in nine months!

In July: **DADDY'S HOME** Kristin James
Naomi Horton
Mary Lynn Baxter

Daddy's Home...and his presence is long overdue!

In August: **FORGOTTEN PAST** Barbara Kaye
Pamela Browning
Nancy Martin

Do you dare to create a future if you've forgotten the past?

Available at your favorite retail outlet.

◈ HARLEQUIN®   ▼ Silhouette

Discover the glorious triumph of three
extraordinary couples fueled by a powerful
passion to defy the past in

Lingering Shadows

The dramatic story of six fascinating men and
women who find the strength to step out of the
shadows and into the light of a passionate future.

Linked by relentless ambition and by desire, each
must confront private demons in a riveting struggle
for power. Together they must find the strength to
emerge from the lingering shadows of the past, into
the dawning promise of the future.

Look for this powerful new blockbuster by *New
York Times* bestselling author

PENNY JORDAN

Available in August at your favorite retail outlet.

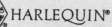

Fifty red-blooded, white-hot, true-blue hunks from every State in the Union!

Beginning in May, look for MEN MADE IN AMERICA! Written by some of our most popular authors, these stories feature fifty of the strongest, sexiest men, each from a different state in the union!

Two titles available every other month at your favorite retail outlet.

In July, look for:

CALL IT DESTINY by Jayne Ann Krentz (Arizona)
ANOTHER KIND OF LOVE by Mary Lynn Baxter (Arkansas)

In September, look for:

DECEPTIONS by Annette Broadrick (California)
STORMWALKER by Dallas Schulze (Colorado)

You won't be able to resist MEN MADE IN AMERICA!